SKY SABOTAGE

SKY SABOTAGE

Franklin W. Dixon

Illustrated by Paul Frame

from the
library
of

David Black

WANDERER BOOKS

Published by Simon & Schuster, Inc., New York

The author wishes to thank Dr. Douglas D. Lloyd
for his expert advice on satellites.

Copyright © 1983 by Simon & Schuster, Inc.
All rights reserved
including the right of reproduction
in whole or in part in any form
Published by WANDERER BOOKS, A Division of
Simon & Schuster, Inc.
Simon & Schuster Building
1230 Avenue of the Americas
New York, New York 10020

Manufactured in the United States of America
10 9 8 7 6 5 4 3 2
10 9 8 7 6 5 4 3   pbk
THE HARDY BOYS, WANDERER and colophon
are registered trademarks of Simon & Schuster, Inc.

Library of Congress Cataloging in Publication Data
Dixon, Franklin W.
Sky sabotage.

(The Hardy boys mystery stories; 79)
Summary: Frank and Joe go to Florida to investigate
the sabotage of a satellite launch and uncover a theft
ring involving sea animals.
[1. Mystery and detective stories] I. Frame, Paul
ill. II. Title.   III. Series: Dixon,
Franklin W. Hardy boys mystery stories; 79.
PZ7.D644Sk 1982   [Fic]   83-1240
ISBN 0-671-47556-8
ISBN 0-671-47557-6 (pbk.)

Contents

1 The Glowing Orb

The summer sun hung lazily in the sky over Bayport High School as Joe Hardy swung his yellow sports sedan into the parking lot. It was mid-August and only a few cars were there, belonging either to the maintenance crew or the small group of students taking summer school classes. Chet Morton, whom Joe had come to pick up, was one of them.

Joe parked and switched off his motor. He glanced at his watch and grunted. Chet's math class would not be finished for another fifteen minutes. With a sigh, he brushed a clump of blond hair off his forehead and lay down on the car seat to take a short nap. He closed his eyes and began to think of the evening ahead. Should he make a date with his girlfriend, Iola Morton? Or go to the movies? His thoughts soon began to drift and seconds later he was dozing peacefully.

Joe's eyes flickered open as he heard a car pull alongside his in the lot. He listened for a door to open and someone to get out. But nothing happened.

A moment later, another car pulled up. This time, Joe heard a door open and shut, and the sound of footsteps coming nearer. Then the car next to him opened and closed.

Suddenly, a rough, masculine voice broke the silence. It had a gravelly, no-nonsense sound, and Joe could hear it clearly through the open windows.

"I hope you have the money!"

"Shhh!" another man warned. He sounded high-pitched and nervous.

"Nobody's around here," the first man retorted without lowering his volume. "Where's the money?"

Joe, listening intently by now, heard an envelope being torn open, then the shuffle of papers. Whatever was happening, he realized, was not an ordinary business deal.

"Okay," the rough-voiced man said. "This is

half of it. I want to see the other half as soon as I'm done. Understand?"

"We have no intention of double-crossing you," came the reply. "You just do your job and we'll pay you according to our agreement."

There was a short pause; then the man continued. "You'll have to leave soon. Do you have everything ready for your trip?"

"That's none of your business," the rough-sounding man declared. "The less you know about it, the better. So don't ask any more stupid questions."

Just then, Joe felt a sneeze coming on. The pollen count was unusually high this time of year, and although he didn't normally suffer from hay fever, he had been having a number of sneezing fits that day. Frantically, he covered his nose and mouth with his hands to stifle the attack.

The sneeze, when it came, sounded like a strangled snort.

VRRRROOOOOOOOM!

At the same instant, the car next to him started up, covering the sound. Joe sighed in relief, then listened as the door of the other car opened and closed. A moment later, it too started up and both vehicles began to back out.

Joe lifted his head and watched as the cars

drove from the lot. One was a beige, late-model Ford, the other an older sedan with a white body and a red vinyl top. Quickly he jotted down both license plate numbers. Then he sneezed, again and again.

"Hey, are you all right?" Chet Morton called out as he walked toward Joe's car and spotted his sniffling friend.

Joe sneezed once more before answering. "I'm great. And I have a new mystery to solve."

Chet's face broke into a broad grin. He often helped the amateur detective and his brother Frank solve mysteries, and was always excited over the prospect of a new one. Quickly he squeezed his ample bulk into the passenger seat.

"What's up?" he asked.

Joe started the engine and on their way home told Chet about the two men. Apparently they had chosen the school parking lot to meet surreptitiously. From the way they had spoken, it was clear that one of them was paying the other for an illegal operation, involving a trip and a lot of money.

"I'm going to trace the license numbers and find out who owns those cars," Joe concluded as he pulled up in front of his house. "First, though, I want to tell Frank and Dad about it."

Both his eighteen-year-old brother and his

father were home when Joe and Chet walked in the door. Fenton Hardy was a widely known investigator who had retired from the New York Police Department a long time ago and was now running his own agency in Bayport.

Seventeen-year-old Joe and his dark-haired brother had learned the business from him and had already built up a reputation for themselves.

After hearing what happened, Fenton Hardy dialed the state police and reported the license numbers of both cars. He waited as they were run through the computer. Frank, Joe, and Chet clustered around his desk, anxious for the results.

"The sedan belongs to a man named Ralph Guiamo," the detective announced at last, cupping his hand over the receiver. "He's an ex-convict who spent five years at Leavenworth prison for armed robbery. He's said to be a weapons expert."

"I bet that was the guy with the rough voice," Joe said. "The one who was getting paid."

"What about the other man?" Frank asked excitedly.

"The police are working on that," Mr. Hardy said. "It'll be another—shh!" He waved for the boys to be quiet as he listened to the person on the other end. Suddenly he sat upright in his chair. Then he jumped to his feet and started pacing back and forth, the phone in his left hand.

"Are you sure that's his name?" he asked, then pulled a pad and paper from his top drawer to write something down. Finally he hung up.

"Who is it, Dad?" Frank and Joe nearly shouted, bursting with curiosity.

"The beige Ford belongs to Brad Patterson, one of the top executives for Megavision," Mr. Hardy said.

The boys looked baffled.

"I've been investigating Megavision, which operates communications satellites from their earth stations," Mr. Hardy went on. "It is believed that the company is engaging in ruthless methods to monopolize the market. Several competing firms have gathered to investigate Megavision. They hired me to work on the case, but so far I've found no solid evidence with which to take Megavision to court. My findings, though, lead me to believe that the accusations are true."

"This could be just the break you need, then," Joe said.

"Exactly," his father said, and sat down at his

desk again. "Obviously, Patterson has hired that ex-convict, Guiamo, for something illegal. The police gave me Guiamo's address. He lives outside of Bayport. I want you boys to go there as soon as you can and watch the place."

"We'll leave right now," Joe offered and held out his hand for the piece of paper with the address.

"Not so fast!" a stern, female voice came from behind them. "You two aren't leaving this house without a good dinner in your stomachs."

Frank and Joe groaned. But they knew there was no point in trying to argue with Aunt Gertrude, who stood at the door with her hands on her hips.

"Dinner will be ready in five minutes," she declared. "Now go and wash your hands." Aunt Gertrude, who lived with the Hardy family, had long ago decided that her firm hand was needed in bringing up the boys. But deep inside she was very fond of her nephews and proud of their accomplishments.

"Do you have enough for me, too?" Chet piped up. "My mother isn't home today and I have to eat leftovers." Chet, whose chubby figure attested to his love for food, looked pleadingly at Aunt Gertrude.

She couldn't help but smile. "All right," she

said. "But you're only getting one dessert, just like everybody else!"

After dinner, the boys took Chet home, then drove out of Bayport into the surrounding countryside. They found Ralph Guiamo's house along a deserted stretch of road. It was a small, rundown-looking bungalow.

Frank parked some distance away, and they circled through the woods to the house. No lights were on inside, and the white and red sedan was nowhere to be seen.

"He's not home," Joe remarked. "Maybe he's already left on his trip."

"And maybe he hasn't," Frank said, trying to be optimistic. But a sinking feeling in his stomach told him that their suspect might have slipped away. If Guiamo had already gone on his mission, they might never be able to pin anything on him or Megavision.

"Let's take a look around," he said, stepping from the woods. "Maybe we'll find some clues."

Joe searched the grounds behind Guiamo's house while Frank studied tire tracks in the dirt driveway. Only one car had been there, but its treads were a common type with some wear on the inside. Luckily, however, there was a distinguishing S-shaped gouge on the left rear tire.

15

Joe found nothing of interest and soon it was too dark to look anymore. The boys sat in the bushes and waited, hoping the ex-convict would show up. In an hour, the stars came out and a warm night breeze swayed the tops of the trees. Sill there was no sign of Guiamo.

"Hey! What's that?" Joe blurted suddenly as he stared into the distance. He sprang to his feet and pointed toward the dark sky near the horizon. "It looks like a flying saucer!"

"A what?" Frank asked. Then his eyes grew wide as he saw what Joe was pointing to. A glowing, silvery orb hung motionless in the sky about a mile away. Then it began to rise slowly.

"What is it?" Joe stammered, not really believing it was an alien space ship.

"I don't know," Frank replied. "But if ever there was a UFO, this is one."

Joe knew that thousands of sightings were reported every year by people around the world who usually believed them to be flying saucers from outer space. This had never been proven, but many of the strange occurrences had never been explained, either.

"It looks as if it just took off," Frank said. "Let's see if we can find the spot where it started from."

The Hardys raced back to their car. Joe drove

16

as Frank kept his eye on the UFO, trying to locate the spot directly beneath it.

"Turn right here," he commanded, indicating an overgrown dirt road that led through the woods up a hill. "It's just past this—"

KERBLAMMMMM!

A loud explosion ripped through the night air and a bright flash of light illuminated the sky for a fraction of a second. Then the UFO vanished!

2 Trouble in Florida

"It blew up!" Joe cried in amazement.

He stoped the car and searched the sky, but saw nothing but the moon and the stars. The glowing silver orb was gone.

"That's bizarre!" Frank called out, his face etched with wonder. "What'll we do now?"

"Keep going," Joe urged, now more intrigued than ever. "Maybe fragments of the thing fell to the ground."

Continuing along the dirt road, the boys finally arrived at a large cornfield. Convinced this was where the UFO had been hovering, they stopped and took flashlights out of the glove compartment. Then they went into the field, looking for debris of the UFO. After twenty minutes of unrewarded search, they returned to the car.

"We'll have to come back in the morning when it's light," Frank said, glancing once more at the sky above. "Maybe we'll spot something then."

Joe nodded. "Let's go back to Guiamo's place. He may be there by now."

"Hey, look!" Frank exclaimed suddenly, shining his flashlight on the dirt road. "Tire tracks!"

Both boys bent down and studied the marks.

"These are from Guiamo's sedan!" Joe cried out, identifying the S-shaped gouge in one of the threads. "And they're fresh!"

Frank nodded. "Let's get back to his house," he urged. "If Guiamo's there, we may be able to clear this mystery up."

The Hardys climbed into their car and drove off. Soon they arrived at the small bungalow. It was still dark inside and the white and red sedan was not there.

Frank sighed. "Would you mind if I dropped you off here to watch the house? I want to go home and talk this over with Dad."

"Go ahead," the blond boy said. "And while you're there, pick up a couple of sleeping bags. We may be here all night."

"Good idea."

Joe hid in the bushes and Frank drove off. Once he was home, the young detective reported the evening's events to his father. Mr. Hardy listened carefully, then sat back in his chair and pondered the situation.

"Spend the night out there if you have to," he decided at last. "If Guiamo doesn't return, I would like you to go to Florida in the morning."

"Florida?" Frank queried, puzzled.

"Yes. Aristo, one of Megavision's toughest competitors, is planning to launch a communications satellite from Cape Canaveral tomorrow night. If that launch were somehow interrupted, it would be a major blow to Aristo."

"Do you think Megavision is planning to sabotage the launch?" Frank asked, his eyes growing wide.

"Could be," Mr. Hardy replied. "We know that Guiamo is a weapons expert and that he's going on a trip."

Frank let out a low whistle. Cape Canaveral, on Florida's Atlantic coast, was the site of the Kennedy Space Center, from which many astronauts had been launched into space during the early years of the United States Space Program. Now the site was more often used to send satellites into orbit.

The purposes of the satellites ranged from weather and defense surveillance to global telecommunications, and the cost of building and launching them was enormous. If Aristo's satellite were sabotaged, the loss would be in the multi-million dollar category, and could well put the company out of business.

Fenton Hardy swiveled in his desk chair. "If Guiamo isn't home by early morning, come back here by seven," he said. "I've contacted the Space Center and warned them of the possible trouble ahead. The security there is very tight, but if Guiamo is planning to sabotage the launch, he may have found some way around it. I'll book you on the nine o'clock flight to Orlando."

"Okay, Dad," Frank said. Then he went into his bedroom, where he pulled two sleeping bags out of the closet. A short while later he was on his way back to Guiamo's.

"Still no sign of him?" he asked his brother when he found him in a clump of bushes outside the ex-convict's house.

"No," Joe shrugged. "And I bet . . . *ah-chooo* . . . *ah-chhhooooo* . . ." He burst into a sneezing fit. Since he'd been out in the country, his hay fever had grown worse. His eyes were bloodshot and watery, and his head was clogged and stuffy. "And I bet he won't be back," he finished.

"You're probably right," Frank remarked. Quickly he told about their father's plan to send them to Cape Canaveral.

Joe's watery eyes lit up. "Do you think the air in Florida is better—for my hay fever, I mean?"

Frank laughed. "We'll see. Now why don't you try to get some rest. I'll take the first watch."

Snuggling up in his sleeping bag, Joe had fitful dreams between sneezing attacks. Around midnight he felt his brother's hand shaking him awake.

"My turn so soon?" he complained. "I was just getting to—"

"Shh!" Frank hushed him. "Somebody's coming!"

Joe sat up and listened. Footsteps crunched through the woods behind them. Since they were advancing toward the boys, both prepared to defend themselves.

"Frank! Joe!" a youthful voice called out in a hushed tone. "Where are you?"

"Chet!" Frank replied, recognizing the voice. "What are you doing here?"

Their chubby friend trudged toward them. "Hope I didn't scare you guys," he apologized. "Your dad called me after Frank left. He asked me to tell you that he booked a flight to Florida at eight in the morning, not nine, and wanted to make sure you got home in time to catch it."

"You did alarm us a little," Joe admitted. "But thanks for coming."

Chet's expression turned inquisitive. "What's going on in Florida?"

Frank related his father's theory about the possible sabotage attempt and Chet's jaw dropped. "Boy, I wish I could come, too. But summer school isn't over until for a couple of days."

"I think we can manage without you." Frank chuckled. "But seriously, we're sorry you can't come."

Chet was glum at the thought of missing out on one of the Hardys' adventures. Grumbling over his summer school class, he turned and walked back through the woods to his car.

By dawn, Guiamo still had not returned to his house and the boys gave up waiting. Before going back to town, though, they stopped at the cornfield and searched once more for debris from the exploded UFO.

"Here's something!" Frank said, stooping down between two rows of corn. He picked up a foot-long piece of shredded plastic. From the writing on it, he quickly deduced that it was from a weather balloon. "So that's what our mysterious UFO was," he smiled. "A weather balloon."

"But why was it lit up like that?" Joe wondered. "Why did it blow up? And what was it doing here?"

The older boy looked thoughtful. "I have no idea."

When they arrived home, the Hardys found their father making breakfast.

"Mr. Stone, head of Security at the Space Center, will pick you up at the airport," Mr. Hardy informed them, dishing scrambled eggs onto their plates. "He'll fill you in on anything you need to know. I also got you a photograph of Guiamo. It was taken years ago when he was sent to prison, but it still ought to be a good likeness. Here it is."

Frank took the photo, studied it a moment, and placed it in his pocket. He and Joe finished their eggs, packed their clothes, and drove to the airport. Three hours later, they were standing outside the terminal in Orlando.

Joe took a deep breath of the Florida air, then exhaled. "I think I'm going to like it here." He grinned. "My hay fever is disappearing already."

The boys heard a horn toot and saw a hand waving at them from an official-looking dark gray sedan. It had SPACE CENTER SECURITY inscribed on its door.

"That must be Mr. Stone," Frank said, returning the wave and picking up his suitcase.

The head of Space Center security was a stocky man with bulging eyes. "Welcome to the sunshine state," he beamed as he grabbed the youths' luggage and stuffed it into his trunk. He slammed the lid shut and extended a big right hand. "We've heard a lot about Fenton Hardy and his two sons down here."

Joe shook the extended hand. "I'm Joe." He smiled. "This is my brother, Frank."

Once introductions were over and the group on their way to the Space Center, Mr. Stone's cheerful manner subsided. He explained that security had been tightened around the Space Center since Mr. Hardy had called. It would now be very difficult for any stranger to penetrate it without being caught.

"Unless this guy Guiamo is invisible," Mr.

Stone remarked, "he won't get near the place."

"How close *can* someone get to the launch?" Frank inquired.

"Oh, a few miles. But I have men watching the whole Cape to see who comes and goes. They'll check out anyone who isn't there for a good reason."

"Where is your weakest point?" Joe asked.

"The ocean off Cocoa Beach. A lot of boats collect there to watch, and it's hard to control their coming and going."

"And what time is the satellite due to be launched?" Frank took over again.

"It's supposed to go off at nine tonight."

The dark-haired sleuth checked his watch. If Guiamo was going to sabotage the launch, there wasn't much time left to track him down. "Can you get us an unmarked car and a list of marinas in the area?" he asked.

"No problem." The security man nodded. "What do you have in mind?"

"I have a hunch that Guiamo is planning to shoot down the rocket carrying the satellite from a point in the ocean!" Frank declared.

3 Sabotage

The security man shook his head. "You can't just shoot a big space rocket with a rifle!" he objected.

"Of course you can't," Frank agreed. "But we saw something strange last night that might have been a trial run for this. A huge weather balloon was blown up. We don't know from what distance, but it disintegrated almost completely, leaving only a small piece of debris. Obviously whoever did it had some pretty sophisticated equipment."

"The explosion was near Guiamo's house," Joe added. "And he's a weapons expert."

"You might have something there," the security head agreed, finally bringing his car to a stop in front of one of the scattered buildings in the Space Center.

Frank and Joe waited in the parking area while Mr. Stone went inside. In the distance, they could see the rocket on the launch pad, final preparations being made for its departure. In a few minutes, Stone returned and handed them the keys to an unmarked Ford station wagon. He also gave them a list of nearby marinas.

"Good luck," he said. "If you come up with anything, contact the Coast Guard. I'll call them, so they'll be ready if you need help."

Frank and Joe drove away and soon were making their round of marinas. The first three places they visited didn't pay off. The fourth one did.

"It could've been him," a lanky old dockmaster said, scratching his head and staring at the photograph Frank had given him. "But he looks a lot younger in the picture. His hair is different, too."

"Did you see what kind of car he was driving?" Joe asked with mounting excitement in his voice.

"No. Someone dropped him off. He paid in cash too, five-hundred-dollar deposit plus rent on the boat. Said his name was Barker."

"Probably fake," Joe mumbled to himself, then asked the dockmaster for a description of the rented boat.

"It's a forty-foot cruiser," the man replied, "named *Beachcomber*. The fellow took it out late this morning."

"We'd like to rent a boat, too," Frank said. "Do you have any left?"

"Just that one there," the lanky dockmaster told him, pointing to a skiff with a powerful outboard engine.

"We'll take it."

The boys paid a deposit on the skiff, then zoomed off with full throttle toward the nearest inlet. The tiny craft was not built for ocean travel. It bounced dangerously over the choppy waves that rolled in the inlet's entrance. But once they were outside the chop, the skiff handled well in the gentle ocean swells. Frank turned up the coast toward Cocoa Beach.

From the dockmaster's hazy identification of Guiamo, neither boy was totally confident that the ex-convict was the one who had rented the forty-foot cruiser. But with time running out they had to take the chance that it was.

"Why do you think he was dropped off?" Joe shouted from the bow.

"Maybe he didn't want to be seen loading his

equipment," Frank replied. "He probably met a partner somewhere along the shore later and transferred the stuff there."

Frank continued steering the skiff up the coast. It was already late in the afternoon and the Florida sun was dropping slowly in the sky. In the distance, the huge rocket and the Space Center launch tower were clearly visible. But the boys were still miles away from it. It was not until the sun was hanging like a bright orange ball just above the horizon that they spotted a cluster of boats anchored off Cocoa Beach.

"There must be at least fifty of them!" Joe cried. "We can't check them all!"

Frank smiled. "We don't have to. I think I see it already."

Set apart from the other craft was a long cabin cruiser. Frank had figured that Guiamo would anchor away from the crowd, and so he felt confident that this was the *Beachcomber*. He turned the skiff toward the cruiser.

"Maybe we ought to call the Coast Guard," Joe remarked. "Guiamo could blow us out of the water if he wanted."

"We will," Frank said tersely. "But first I want to make sure that it's the right boat and that Guiamo is on it."

Frank maneuvered the skiff toward the cruiser, coming close enough to read its name on the stern. It was, indeed, called *Beachcomber*. But there was no one on deck.

"We'll have to draw him out without making him suspicious," Joe said.

"Let's pretend we're out of gas," Frank suggested. "We'll hail him for help."

"Good idea."

Frank motored up to the cruiser, and then cut off the fuel feed line to the outboard engines. Soon they sputtered to a stop.

"Help! Help!" the two boys started yelling. "We're out of gas. Help!" They waved and shouted for over a minute with no response. Finally a man stepped on the cruiser's deck. He was too far away for them to recognize.

"We're out of gas," Joe shouted. "Can you help us?"

The man hesitated. Then he disappeared into his cabin again. A moment later, the cruiser's engines started up.

"He fell for it!" Frank said excitedly. "Apparently he was afraid other people around us would take notice."

They watched as the *Beachcomber* moved in their direction. Soon it pulled alongside the skiff and its captain came on deck again. He had a large, curving nose and a pockmarked complexion. Frank and Joe felt sure he was the ex-convict Ralph Guiamo.

"Idiots. You shouldn't even be out here in that thing," he grunted.

Joe recognized the rough-sounding voice he had overheard in the high school parking lot.

"We got lost," the young detective explained. "We couldn't find the inlet and now we're out of gas. If you could spare us a little and point us toward the inlet, we'd really appreciate it. We'll pay you for the fuel, of course."

"Idiots." The man grunted again and turned to go back into his cabin. "I'll check below."

Once Guiamo was out of sight, Joe whispered to his brother that now might be a good chance to board the cruiser. But Frank shook his head. "I saw a bulge in Guiamo's jacket," he replied. "I think he's got a gun."

Guiamo emerged again, looking agitated. "My engine runs on diesel fuel. So even if I could drain some from my tank, it wouldn't work with your outboard."

"Do you mind if we use your radio to call the Coast Guard?" Frank asked. "They could bring us some gas."

The surly ex-convict nearly jumped at the

suggestion. "No!" he snapped. "My radio doesn't work."

"Then would you tow us to shore when you leave?" Joe pressed. "We don't mind waiting."

Guiamo began pacing the cruiser's deck like a caged animal. His eyes scanned the water.

The nearest other boat was about two hundred yards away. The sun was just touching the horizon, and in a few minutes it would be dark. He unconsciously fondled the bulge in his jacket, then glared at the stranded youths in the skiff. Frank and Joe knew they were treading on thin ice.

"Let me check below one more time," Guiamo replied at last. "There might be a gas can stowed somewhere for the outboard motor on my dinghy."

"Thanks," Joe smiled as the man returned to his cabin.

Guiamo was clearly stalling for time. Once it was dark, he could handle his unwanted visitors without danger of being noticed by the other boats. He might just motor away to a new spot, leaving the youths stranded, or invite Frank and Joe aboard to deal with them at gunpoint. There would be no witnesses. Just two foolish teenagers lost at sea.

The boys had not wanted to arouse Guiamo's suspicions, but at this point things looked risky. Without exchanging a word, they went into action. Frank primed the skiff's outboard with gas while Joe wound the starter cord tightly in place. Then he yanked the cord with all his strength.

VVVRRRRROOOOOMMMM . . .

The outboard started without a hitch and he threw it into full throttle. In seconds, they were speeding away from the cruiser. Frank looked back to see Guiamo bursting from the cabin. He appeared to draw his gun, then decide against it.

"I wonder what he makes of us," Joe laughed, relieved that their escape had been successful.

"I don't know," Frank said. "But we shouldn't give him too much time to think about it."

The sun was now gone. The rocket carrying the satellite was silhouetted against the sky several miles in the distance, standing like a great monument over the sands of Cocoa Beach. The launch was due to take place in one hour.

Joe aimed the skiff at full speed toward a large cruiser, and soon the two boys were explaining to an elderly man and woman that they had to make an emergency radio call. The couple let them come aboard, and minutes later about five Coast Guard vessels were advancing toward Guiamo's rented cruiser. There was still enough light left in the sky for the boys to see that the ex-convict made no attempt to escape.

"He knows he's trapped," Joe commented, peering through a pair of binoculars that the elderly couple kept on board. "He's giving up."

But just before the Coast Guard vessels were ready to surround the *Beachcomber*, Joe spotted Guiamo dropping a large, heavy object into the water on the other side.

"He's throwing something overboard!" the blond boy cried.

"Getting rid of the evidence, I bet," Frank put in. "Let's tell the Coast Guard. Maybe they have a diver among them."

Thanking the old man and woman for their help, Frank and Joe climbed back into their skiff and returned to Guiamo's cruiser. By the time they boarded the *Beachcomber*, two Coast Guard officers were already questioning the man.

The others were searching the boat for signs of a sabotage attempt. But they came up with nothing. Guiamo sat in a corner of the cabin.

"So those are the guys who contacted you," he said to the lieutenant in charge, eyeing the boys with hostility. "I don't know how they got that crazy notion that I was some kind of saboteur. I suppose they're just kids with over-active imaginations."

The lieutenant, a tall man with short, wavy hair and a big Adam's apple, looked doubtfully at the Hardys. "Mr. Stone at the Space Center said you two were top-notch detectives and we were to back you up. But frankly, I think you're way off base here."

"I agree," another officer put in. "Mr. Guiamo says he's here on vacation, and so far we've found nothing to support this sabotage suspicion of yours."

"We saw him drop something large over-board before you surrounded him," Frank spoke up. "If you could send a diver down to get it, you may find that our notion isn't crazy at all."

At first, the lieutenant was doubtful. But Frank and Joe were so persuasive that finally he gave in. Since they were near the shore, the water wasn't very deep, and as he did have equipment handy, the lieutenant sent a diver down. Guiamo still acted as if the whole idea was insane, but he was beginning to sweat.

Th scuba diver was under water for ten minutes before he bobbed to the surface. "Give me a line!" he shouted. "I found something!"

Excited, the boys watched as several large objects were hauled onto the deck. Two were miniature missiles, no more than two feet long. The third was a launcher for the missiles.

Guiamo groaned. "Stupid punks!" he hissed at the Hardys. "This whole job would've gone like clockwork if it hadn't been for you. How did you know, anyway?"

The boys did not answer. They just smiled as the Coast Guard lieutenant exclaimed, "This is incredible! Mr. Guiamo, you're under arrest!"

4 Blast-off

In a moment Guiamo was handcuffed, and the lieutenant extended a hand to Frank and Joe. "I owe you boys an apology," he said. "It never occurred to me that a civilian would be able to get his hands on this kind of equipment."

"How does it work?" Joe asked.

"These are special heat-seeking missiles," the officer explained. "All you have to do is shoot them in the general direction of a heat source, and their sensors will pick it up."

"And the rocket carrying the satellite sure is a heat source!" Joe put in.

The officer nodded. "You boys prevented a real catastrophe this evening."

Joe looked at his watch. It was nine o'clock. "It's blast-off time, isn't it?" he asked.

"Not yet," the lieutenant said. "The launch was delayed when we received your message. But I'll radio Space Center now and tell them to resume the countdown. Maybe you can get back in time to watch from the control room."

"That would be great!" Frank exclaimed.

The Coast Guard hoisted the Hardys' rented skiff aboard one of their boats, offering to return it to the marina for them in the morning. Another boat took Guimao's cruiser in tow. A third vessel was used to transport the saboteur and his mini heat-seeking missiles.

Once back on dry land, Frank and Joe were quickly escorted to a waiting car and driven to the Space Center.

"Well, I never would've guessed," Mr. Stone cried with admiration as he greeted them.

"We had a hard time believing it ourselves," Joe admitted with a smile. "But now we know what lighted up the weather balloon last night. Guiamo had rigged up some sort of heat source inside that caused it to glow."

"You're probably right," Mr. Stone agreed.

They entered the control room, where technicians were busily making last-minute checks on the upcoming launch. When they saw the boys, they gave them a round of applause for thwarting the sabotage attempt. Several people left their stations for a moment to shake hands with the Hardys and congratulate them.

A woman appeared from an adjoining room and walked briskly up to them. She appeared to be in her mid-thirties and had a pretty face.

"I don't have time to talk right now," she said as she stopped in front of them. "But please wait here after the launch. I want to discuss something with you. It's important!"

Before Frank and Joe could utter a word in reply, she was hurrying back to her post.

The young detectives looked at each other somewhat bewildered, then turned their attention again to the control room.

"Follow me," Mr. Stone said with a jerk of his head. "We'll go to the observation deck to watch the blast-off. It's quite something."

Never having seen a space launch other than on TV, Frank and Joe eagerly followed the security man to a special window. A group of important-looking men were seated in front of it.

"T minus twenty seconds and counting," a loudspeaker announced.

All eyes were fixed on the huge rocket as the countdown went into the final ten seconds.

"Ten. Nine. Eight. Seven. Six. Five. Four. Three. Two. One. Lift-off . . ."

Bright flames and smoke shot out from beneath the rocket, lighting up the night. A second later, it left the launch pad.

"We have lift-off!" the loudspeaker announced.

The Hardys blinked in awe as they saw the rocket soar upward, propelled by a shaft of blazing fuel. A moment later it was high in the sky and well on its way into space.

"It's amazing!" Joe breathed at last.

Just then a telephone rang in the observation room. One of the men picked it up. "Long distance for Frank or Joe Hardy," he called out.

Joe took the receiver. "Dad!" he said, recognizing his father's voice. "Did you hear what happened?"

"Yes," Fenton Hardy chuckled over the line. "And I'm very proud of you both. Not only did you prevent the sabotage, but we now have a good case against Megavision. Between overhearing the two men in the high school parking lot, and then catching Guiamo red-handed, I think we can put that company out of business for good."

"Great!" Joe exclaimed.

"Great and not so great," his father said.

"Megavision is a ruthless organization. That's been demonstrated. And now they'll be fighting for their lives."

Joe's smile dropped from his face. "I see what you mean. Since I'm the one who overheard the conversation between the Megavision executive and Guiamo, I'll be an important witness in the trial against them."

"You'll be the only one who can tie them together," Mr. Hardy confirmed. "Without you, there may be no way to prove that Guiamo was hired by Megavision. So be very careful. Star witnesses often have fatal 'accidents' before they can testify."

Joe gulped. "Does Megavision know about me?"

"I can't say," the famous detective replied. "I've told the police to keep it a secret, but I can't be positive that something hasn't already leaked out. So keep your eyes open!"

Stunned, Joe hung up the phone and relayed his conversation with their father to Frank.

"I'll make sure nothing happens to you," the dark-haired boy said, trying to sound cheerful. "After all, we can't lose our star witness, now can we? And who could I pick on if I didn't have my baby brother around?"

Joe smiled thinly at his brother's kidding.

"Okay, I'm in your hands. So where do we sleep tonight?"

"We'll take a room at a nearby motel," Frank decided. "Let's get our luggage from Mr. Stone."

"That reminds me," Joe said, slapping his forehead. "We left the car he gave us at the marina. We'll have to get that, too."

The boys went to look for the security chief, who was in the control room. He offered to have the car picked up and told them their bags were at the reception desk.

They had just turned to leave the room when a voice called out, "Oh, there you are!"

The pretty technician who had spoken to them earlier was walking toward them. The boys had completely forgotten about her!

"I'm glad I caught you," she said. "I'm Maggie Russell. When I heard how you foiled that sabotage attempt, I knew I had to talk to you."

"Does it have something to do with the launch?" Joe asked, studying her closely. She had auburn hair, a button nose, and dimpled cheeks. But her face showed signs of worry and lack of sleep. Her brown eyes were rimmed with redness, and they had a glazed, distant look about them.

"No," Maggie replied. "It has nothing to do

with the satellite. It's personal." Her lips began to quiver as she continued. "You see, somebody kidnapped my Sam and Samantha! And they won't give them back, and Samantha is only two, and . . . and . . ." At this point, tears began to form in her eyes and she couldn't go on.

Frank felt a rush of sympathy for the woman. "Have you contacted the police yet?" he asked.

"Yes, yes, I told the police," Maggie choked through her tears. "But nobody seems to take it very seriously. So I thought maybe you could help me."

"Somebody kidnapped your children and the police won't take it seriously?" Joe asked in disbelief.

Maggie's face glowed red with embarrassment. "Oh, I'm sorry," she sniffled, looking down at the floor. "Sam and Samantha aren't my children, although sometimes I feel like they are. They're my two pet porpoises."

"Your what?" the blond boy blurted.

"Porpoises," the woman stammered. "I . . . I know it sounds silly, but they're the only things that ever really mattered to me, at least since my husband died several years ago. You see, we never had any children, so I started raising porpoises to . . ." Her voice trailed off and the distant look appeared again in her eyes.

Upon hearing that Sam and Samantha were only porpoises, Frank and Joe were so relieved they had to bite their lips to keep from laughing. But they were glad they did. To this woman, her pets were the children she'd never had, and now they were gone.

"And you say somebody kidnapped them?" Frank asked.

"Yes," Maggie replied, now more composed. "A couple of days ago I went home from work and found Sam and Samantha missing. I keep them in a lagoon next to my beach house. When I saw that they were gone, I nearly went out of my mind. I contacted the police and they sent someone to look around. But he didn't come up with anything. The next day I got a note in the mail from the kidnapper. It told me to go to an empty lot at three that afternoon and to bring five thousand dollars' ransom. I did. But nobody met me to take the money, and Sam and Samantha are still missing."

"And you want us to help you find them," Joe said, completing her thought.

Maggie nodded. "Please, could you?" she begged, her big, brown eyes imploring the young detectives.

The brothers glanced at each other. "We'll try," Frank promised.

46

Her face brightened. "You can live in my house while you're working on the case," she offered.

"Thanks," Frank said. "We'll take you up on that invitation."

On the way out of the Space Center, Frank stopped at a public telephone to tell their father their plans. Then he and Joe followed Maggie to her car.

Soon they were driving down the coast. By the time they arrived at her beach house, both boys were very tired.

"You'd better get some sleep," Maggie advised. "I'll fix you pancakes in the morning."

"Hey!" Joe suddenly cried out. "There's someone in the bushes!"

5 *Shocked!*

Frank glanced at a clump of shrubbery on the side of the beach house. A dark figure was hunched behind it, barely visible through the leaves.

"Don't look at him," the young detective said in a hushed voice to his brother. "We don't want to scare him off."

Pretending not to see the prowler, the boys calmly took their bags out of the trunk and walked toward the front door. Once they were hidden from the stranger's view, they put down their luggage and moved in opposite directions.

Pressing his body to the wall, Frank stealthily worked his way to the corner. Joe circled around the house. When they were ready to spring into action, they signaled each other with a bird call. Then they converged on the bushes at the same moment!

Joe dove into the shrubs, landing a flying tackle on the prowler.

"OOOOfffff!" the stranger cried as the wind was knocked out of him. Then both boys grabbed him by his arms and dragged him to his feet.

He was a skinny blond boy, no older than Joe, and he seemed scared to death that the brothers were going to hurt him.

"Please let me go!" he begged. "I can explain. I swear!"

"Then explain!" Joe said curtly, relaxing his grip.

"My name is Fred Wardell," the boy began. "I heard that Mrs. Russell's porpoises were stolen, just like my Sparky. I wanted to talk to her, but she wasn't home. So I sat in a beach chair to wait and fell asleep. When I heard the car, I came to meet her. But I heard your voices, so I stayed in the bushes to see what was going on."

"Is Sparky a porpoise, too?" Frank asked.

"No. He's an electric eel. I have a couple of others. Come to my house tomorrow and I'll show them to you."

Maggie had walked up to the group and overheard the boy's story. "I know just how you feel," she said sympathetically. "Other people often don't understand how important pets can be."

"Oh, we understand," Frank said. "But Fred shouldn't prowl around private property at night. It looks awfully suspicious, besides being illegal."

"Oh, I don't mind," Maggie said with a smile. "But he would have scared me if you two hadn't been around."

Fred nodded. "I know. It's just that I've had Sparky for six years, ever since I was a kid. I'm desperate to get him back!"

"Well, Frank and Joe are detectives and are going to find Sam and Samantha," Maggie said. "If the same thieves took Sparky, maybe they'll find him, too!"

"Oh, that would be great!" Fred's eyes sparkled with hope. "You know, there have been a number of recent thefts, some of them pets and all of them sea animals. I don't know what anyone would want with them. But it's been in the papers."

"Have you any idea who the thieves could be?" Joe asked Fred.

"Not really," the boy replied. "But I'm developing some theories. Would you like to come to my house in the morning? We could go over everything, and I could also show you my electric eels."

"Sounds good," Frank said with a smile. Then he yawned. "Right now, though, I want to sleep."

After getting Fred's address, the brothers followed Maggie into her house. She led them to a guest room, and soon they were in bed.

In the morning over breakfast, Maggie showed Frank and Joe the note she'd received about her kidnapped pets. It was written with a felt tip pen in block letters.

"As I told you before," Maggie said, "I went to meet the kidnapper. I waited an hour, but then I had to leave. It was the day before the launch, and there was a lot of work at the Space Center. It was hard enough to take time off as it was. You see, I'm in charge of a computer which monitors the launch functions. I never would've left work if this hadn't been so important."

"Maybe the kidnapper chickened out at the last minute," Joe reflected. "Maybe it was a couple of kids, and they realized that an empty lot at midday is a pretty risky place for such a transaction."

After breakfast, the sleuths borrowed an old pickup truck from Maggie. It was her late husband's and she didn't use it much. There was also a small Honda motorcycle in her garage that she offered the boys if they needed it.

In the pickup, Frank and Joe drove to Fred's house, following the directions he had given them the night before. It was a small home in an inland suburban neighborhood.

"I'm glad you guys made it," the thin boy beamed as he opened the door. He introduced the Hardys to his parents, then led them downstairs to what he called the basement. By northern standards it was not really a basement, the boys realized, since it was mostly above ground with plenty of windows and its own entrance.

"These are my pets," Fred said, pointing to a collection of large tanks. "Cute, aren't they?"

The Hardy boys laughed as they gazed in wonder at the creatures. They were anything but cute. In fact, the electric eels were some of the ugliest things the brothers had ever seen—big, grayish-green aquatic snakes with membranelike fins running from head to tail along the upper and lower portions of their bodies. There were four of them, three of which lay motionless on the floor of their tanks. The fourth was wiggling slowly from one corner of its aquarium to the other.

Fred not only kept the eels as pets, he had been studying their electric charges and had learned to read their electrical signals. The tanks were rigged with metal plates. Wires ran from them to various gauges and other electronic instruments. Fred also knew how to use the eels to power electric appliances, and he gave the young detectives a demonstration by lighting a bulb. Frank and Joe were delighted.

"I've never seen anything like this!" Frank said.

"Sparky was my best eel," Fred said when he had finished his demonstration. "I've been working on him for five years."

"How was he stolen?" Joe asked.

"The thief must have been a real pro," Fred replied, "someone who knew how to handle these things. I came down here one morning, found the door broken, and Sparky gone." He paused a moment, lost in thought. "That's what makes me think it was the same guy who stole Mrs. Russell's porpoises. You need a pro for a job like that, too."

"Who do you think was responsible?" Frank asked.

"Well, I found out that Sealand, a nearby aquarium, reported a string of animal thefts over the past year. It involved porpoises, sharks, and stingrays. So I checked it out."

"What did you find?" Frank inquired.

"I found that after the thefts there security got tighter and tighter. That's why I believe the thieves started picking on private owners."

"Let's go to Sealand," Joe suggested.

"Good idea," Fred said, and told his parents of their plan. Then the three piled into Maggie's pickup and drove to the aquarium. It was one of Florida's biggest attractions, and neither of the Hardys had seen it before.

"First we talk to Mr. Brewster," Fred suggested after they had parked the pickup. "He's one of the managers here and is helping the police in their investigation. He can fill us in on anything new. Then I'll give you a tour of the place. It's worth seeing."

The boys found Mr. Brewster in his office. The manager greeted them cordially. After having heard about the foiled sabotage attempt on the morning news, he was more than happy to have the Hardy boys working on his case.

Mr. Brewster was a short, neat-looking man who took great pride in a job well done. Therefore, he was frustrated to admit that he didn't know much more about the thefts than Fred did. At first, he had thought it was an inside job. But all Sealand employees had been questioned at length about the thefts and seemed innocent. The few who Brewster thought might be capable of doing such a thing had good alibis. He was stumped.

"Do you have a list of the people you wonder about?" Frank asked. "I'd like to double-check their alibis."

Mr. Brewster pulled a piece of paper from his files and handed it to the young detective. Frank looked it over. There were three names on the list.

"Please don't tell anyone about this visit," Joe spoke up. "We don't want these people to know who we are and why we're here."

"Fine," the manager said with a smile. "But get back to me as soon as you come up with an answer."

Leaving Mr. Brewster's office, Frank, Joe, and Fred began their tour of Sealand. Fred led them through the lower level of the main building, which was constructed around a huge center tank filled with porpoises, manta rays, hammerhead sharks, sea tortoises, and other fish.

The boys could see the bottom of the large tank through windows. There also were smaller saltwater aquariums holding strange and rare sea creatures.

"Some of these things look frightening!" Joe said.

"Not when you're used to them," Fred told him. "Now let's go upstairs. On the roof they have shows with trained porpoises and whales."

When they arrived, they found out that the next show would be in an hour. Fred shrugged. "That's all right," he said. "We'll go to the shark canal first and then come back."

The shark canal was in back of the main building. It contained tiger sharks, lemon sharks, nurse sharks, and many others. The boys joined a cluster of visitors on one of the footbridges that crossed over the canal. They leaned over the railing and stared into the water.

"There's a beauty!" Joe exclaimed, pointing to a shark which was easily over twelve feet long.

"That's a man-eater," Fred stated. "They—" He stopped and gasped as both he and Frank saw Joe lurch forward. With a scream, the younger Hardy flew headfirst into the canal, straight at the shark Fred had just pointed out!

6 *The Beach Bum*

A cry of horror rose from the crowd of onlookers. Many of them turned away as Joe hit the water, afraid of what they might see. Others stared in morbid fascination, expecting the hapless boy to be ripped apart in seconds.

Frank was stunned for a moment, then sprang into action. He leaped over the railing and perched at the edge of the canal. Then he leaned over as far as he could and, holding on with one hand, extended the other toward his brother.

"Grab my hand!" he yelled.

Lucky for Joe, the sudden splash had startled the big man-eater and it had dodged away. But now it turned back. Its gray eyes appeared cold and lifeless, and its jaw was open, exposing a set of razor-sharp teeth.

But the little time the startled man-eater had afforded the boy was enough. Joe pushed himself to the surface and swam directly to the bridge, where Frank caught his hand and yanked him up onto dry land.

Soaking wet and in a mild state of shock, Joe barely noticed the cheering crowd of tourists around him. His hands were trembling.

"Are you okay?" Frank asked in a worried voice.

Joe nodded slowly. "Somebody pushed me," he said. "I didn't fall in."

Frank quickly scanned the people on the bridge. "Whoever he was, he's probably gone," he said grimly. "Did you get a look at him?"

"No," Joe replied. "He was behind me."

When the young detective had recovered somewhat from his frightening experience, the boys began to question the visitors, hoping that someone had seen the person who had pushed Joe. But none had. Like Frank and Fred, they had been watching the sharks.

"Maybe it was the same guy who stole Maggie's porpoises," Joe said.

Frank opened his mouth to speak, then stopped. This was a bad time to remind his shaken brother that the Megavision people were probably watching him and trying to dispose of the star witness against them.

"Let's go back to Maggie's so you can change your clothes," the dark-haired detective suggested instead.

"Okay," Joe agreed. "I think I've had enough of Sealand for today."

The trio left and the Hardys dropped Fred off at his home. Then they continued to the beach house, where Joe changed into a dry set of clothing. When he was finished, the boys decided to call Maggie at the Space Center to tell her what happened. When she finally picked up the phone, she sounded harried.

"I'm glad you called!" she said before Frank could say anything about the Sealand episode. "Something terrible has happened!"

"What?"

"We've lost the Aristo satellite!"

"What do you mean, lost it?" Frank asked. "You just put it into orbit."

"I know!" Maggie blurted. "During the launch, everything was working perfectly. But now we can't pick up its signal, nor can we find it on radar."

"Do you have any idea what happened?" Frank queried.

"Some people think the Megavision sabotage

attempt was successful after all, and that Guiamo was only a decoy. The satellite's designer, however, believes it was shot down by a foreign killer satellite."

"The whole thing sounds very strange," Frank said. "We're on our way over." With that, he hung up.

The Hardys rushed outside and got into Maggie's pickup. Moments later they were on their way to the Space Center. When they arrived, they found the control room humming with activity.

Maggie was standing among a cluster of technicians who were discussing the launch and trying to figure out what went wrong.

"I believe it was a foreign killer satellite," a man insisted loudly as the boys joined the group. "My satellite was in perfect operating condition. It tested out without a flaw both before and during the launch. If there had been anything wrong with either the satellite or the rocket, we would have noticed it."

The speaker had curly brown hair and close-set eyes.

"Frank, Joe," Maggie said, "that's Doug Davies, the chief design engineer from the company that built the Aristo satellite. Doug, meet the Hardy boys."

Davies shook hands with the young detectives. "This is a terrible personal blow to me, you understand," he said. "I designed this bird and now it has mysteriously vanished."

Frank nodded. "You must be very upset," he said.

Their conversation was interrupted by another man, who approached Davies with a handful of computer readouts. Maggie pulled the boys aside so they could talk among themselves.

"I think I'd like to call Dad," Joe said. "He might have some ideas."

When Mr. Hardy heard the news, he was as puzzled as his sons. "I'm flying down there as soon as I can," he said after a moment of thought.

"Call Chet and see if he can join us, too," Frank suggested, remembering that summer school was over that day. "We could use him on the porpoise case."

"Okay," Mr. Hardy replied. "Expect us either tonight or in the morning at the latest."

Frank put the phone down and related his conversation to Joe and Maggie.

"What's going to happen next?" he asked the computer technician.

"We've enlisted the help of the Air Force and

their active tracking systems," Maggie replied. "Maybe they can locate the satellite. We've also asked a special scientific observatory to use its laser optics to try to find it. It's small, you know; it would almost fit in the trunk of a car. Possibly conventional tracking systems could miss it. But the laser telescope is so powerful it can locate any orbiting object bigger than a football."

"Is there anything we can do?" Frank asked.

"Not right now," Maggie replied, disconsolate.

"Then let's go back to the porpoise case for a moment," the young detective said. "Do you have any personal enemies, Maggie? Anyone who may hold a grudge against you?"

"Not that I know of," the woman replied slowly, furrowing her brows. "I mean, I don't think everyone loves me, but as far as I'm aware, nobody hates me, either. At least . . ." A distant look appeared in Maggie's eyes as she thought of something. "Wait a second," she said pensively. "There *is* someone. It's been so long I'd almost forgotten about him."

"Who is he?" Joe asked.

"An old man, a hermit who had built a shack on my property several years ago. He became such a nuisance that I had to order him to leave."

"What happened?" Frank queried. "Tell us about this man."

"He used to be a bum in New York City," Maggie went on. "When he got too old to take the cold winters, he came to Florida. I found him one morning, building a shack from driftwood and old boards on the far side of my lagoon. At first, I felt sorry for the old guy and let him stay. But then he got messy, throwing tin cans and empty bottles into the lagoon with my pets. That made me mad, and when I asked him to stop he practically spat at me. So I called the police and had him evicted. He was very bitter about it."

"Do you know where he went after that?" Joe inquired.

"Oh, yes." Maggie smiled. "He moved about a hundred yards down the beach, to someone else's land. I've hardly seen him since. But I was worried for a while that he'd try something nasty. That was over two years ago."

Maggie glanced around the control room. "I'd better get back to work," she said. "But let me know what happens. The old man's name is Lenny, and you'll find his shack a short way up the beach. He's an ornery old guy, so be careful."

The Hardys left the Space Center and drove back to Maggie's house. Before visiting the transplanted New York vagrant, they investigated the lagoon where Maggie had kept her pets. It was about the size of a large pond and was surrounded by thick shrubbery. At its far end it was connected to the ocean by means of a big concrete pipe running through a stretch of beach. A vehicle could easily pull right up to the pond in the dark and not be noticed.

Frank and Joe checked the beach, but if there had been any tire tracks, they were now wiped out by the wind. Then they looked at the concrete pipe leading to the ocean, wondering if the porpoises could've escaped through it. The duct, though, was covered by a steel grate.

"I suppose the police have already been through all this," Joe shrugged. "Let's go see the bum."

As Maggie had said, Lenny's shack was about a hundred yards up the beach, nestled in a grove of palm trees.

The boys found the old hermit sitting against one of its support posts, smoking a corncob pipe and idly gazing out at the ocean. He pretended not to notice the youths at first, but when they mentioned Maggie's pets, he looked at them with surprise.

"Kidnapped, did you say?" Lenny barked. "Sam and Samantha was kidnapped?"

Frank and Joe searched the man's face for signs that his surprise was faked. But his bushy white beard made it hard to read his expression.

"Yes," Joe said evenly. "And we thought you might know something about it."

"Like maybe I was the one who did it?" the vagrant snapped, glaring acidly at the two boys. "Are you calling me a thief? Is that it?"

"We're not calling you anything," Frank replied. "But we do know you have a grudge against Maggie."

The old man got to his feet, eyeing the Hardys as if ready to take them both on. He spat on the sand, then paused for a second before replying. "Against Maggie, yes, I got a grudge," he said hotly. "Against Sam and Samantha, I ain't got nothin'. I *liked* them."

Frank decided not to press it any further. "Okay, okay. We believe you," he spoke soothingly. "But maybe you could help us find the thief. We suspect someone drove to the lagoon by way of the beach last Friday. Did you notice any vehicles up there late at night?"

Lenny thought for a moment. "As a matter of

fact, I did," he said at last. "A lot of dune buggies and stuff go down the beach in the day, but this one was real late at night. Woke me up, going by."

"Did you see what it was?" Joe asked eagerly.

"Was one of those vans everybody's buying these days. I think it was blue."

"Did you see anything else?" Frank inquired.

The old man shook his head. "Just the van."

The boys weren't certain whether Lenny was telling the truth, but they decided that for the moment they'd accept the information. They thanked him and returned to Maggie's beach house, where they had left the pickup.

"Let's go to Sealand and see if any of those people Mr. Brewster mentioned owns a blue van," Frank suggested. Then he added with a wink, "Don't worry. We won't go near the shark canal."

Once the Hardys arrived at the aquarium, they went straight to the personal manager's office.

"I think you're on to something!" Mr. Brewster said when he heard their story. "One of our porpoise trainers owns a blue Chevy van!"

7 *The Grinning Porpoise*

"Who is he?" Frank asked eagerly.

"His name is Skip Adkins," Mr. Brewster replied. "He's one of the people I suspected. A wild sort of fellow. But he had an alibi for every night one of our animals was taken."

"Sometimes the person with the best alibi is the guilty one," Frank said. "He's the one with something to hide, and arranging alibis is one of the oldest tricks in the book."

Mr. Brewster nodded. "Well, Adkins is on the upper deck right now, giving a show. Why don't you take a look at him?"

"Good," Frank said. "We'll do that."

"I'll bet Adkins was the guy who pushed me

in that canal!" Joe said angrily as they climbed the stairs to the upper level. "Just wait till I get ahold of him."

Frank put an arm around his brother's shoulders. "Skip doesn't even know us," he said. "I think Megavision was responsible for that one."

Joe's jaw dropped. "You mean they've already sent men to kill me?"

"I'm afraid so," Frank replied. "You're a great danger to them. So let's both keep our heads down and our eyes open."

Joe continued up the stairs slowly. "I feel like a sitting duck," he murmured. But when they got to the roof and saw the porpoise show in progress, his spirits picked up again.

"That must be Skip," Frank said, pointing to the muscular, sandy-haired man who hosted the show.

Skip Adkins was standing on a platform which stuck out about ten feet over the main tank. Trained porpoises took turns jumping out of the water and nimbly taking fish bits from his outstretched hand. A crowd of onlookers cheered each time.

With nothing better to do than wait, Frank and Joe enjoyed the show. The porpoises flew through hoops and danced on their tails at Skip's command.

"He doesn't seem like the criminal type to me," Joe commented in a whisper.

"Hey, Frank, Joe!" a voice suddenly broke from the crowd. The Hardys turned and spotted Fred Wardell weaving his way toward them through the spectators.

"Mr. Brewster told me I would find you up here," he said excitedly. He had a newspaper tucked under his arm, which he pulled out and began to unfold. "I found something in today's paper. It might be the answer to this whole mystery!"

"Can you meet us on the lower level?" Frank said in a hushed voice. "I don't want us to be seen together right—"

Just then, about a gallon of water hit Fred squarely in the back, drenching him thoroughly.

"Hey! What's the big idea?" he shouted, spinning around in time to see a porpoise flop back into the water behind him.

A second later, it popped to the surface again. It seemed to be grinning, and emitted a strange noise which sounded like laughter.

"That's what you get for turning your back on *my* show," Skip Adkins joked over the loudspeaker, evoking a chorus of laughter from the spectators.

Frank and Joe, who'd caught some of the spray themselves, stared at the muscular man on the platform. Clearly, Skip had seen them talking to Fred and had decided to have a little fun with the boys.

"In a way, I'm glad he did that," Joe said in a low voice, wiping the water from his face with his sleeve. "It makes him look more suspect than ever."

"Suspect?" Fred spoke up, looking bewildered. "What—?"

"Meet us on the lower level," Frank interrupted. "We'll be down in a few minutes."

Fred headed for the stairs while the Hardys stayed to watch the end of the show. Both felt chagrined. It had been a mistake to be seen with Fred at Sealand. Since the boy had been around so much asking questions, Adkins might know who he was and why he was there.

"This may have blown our cover," Joe said. "Unless Adkins's little trick was just a harmless coincidence."

"I doubt it," Frank said. "But there's nothing we can do about it. Come on, let's go."

Leaving the show area, the sleuths took the stairs to Sealand's lower level. It was almost closing time, and they found Fred in the process of drying out the newspaper he'd wanted to show them.

"So what was going on up there?" he blurted. "What's the big secret?"

Frank quickly explained why they were suspicious of Skip Adkins, . . . then asked Fred for his story.

"Look," the boy said, handing over the newspaper and pointing to an article on page three.

The column was headlined *"Smuggler Porpoises Caught."* Frank and Joe eagerly read the report on a Florida smuggling ring which had been using porpoises to carry illegal goods into the country. Apparently, the animals were fitted with special waterproof containers and were trained to home in on the smugglers' hidden cove. After investigating the gang for months, the police finally raided the cove, taking several men into custody. Photographs of the criminals were included in the article.

"This is incredible!" Joe exclaimed after reading it. "Maybe these are the guys who stole Sam and Samantha!"

"Could be," Frank said thoughtfully. "But it doesn't fit in with the ransom note Maggie received. The smugglers weren't interested in kidnapping porpoises, just stealing them. Also, it doesn't tie in with Fred's electric eel."

"Yes, it does!" Fred spoke up excitedly. "That's what caught my attention in the first place. One of these guys visited my house a few days after Sparky was stolen." He pointed to the image of a balding, jowly man who had been identified as one of the smugglers.

"He came with another guy," Fred went on. "They claimed to be eel lovers and asked about the electrical devices I installed in my tanks."

"How did they know about that?" Frank asked.

"Oh, the newspaper had an article about me recently," Fred replied. "That's why I forgot to tell you. But I really had no reason to believe the men were connected with the theft."

Frank and Joe both knew they were on to something big—bigger than they had imagined. But both were unsure about how everything fit together. They started pacing the floor, trying to think of ways to connect the recent flood of information.

Joe suddenly stopped and snapped his fingers. "I've got an idea. What if the smugglers *did* steal Maggie's porpoises? Then, upon hearing about the theft, the old hermit decided to pretend *he* had kidnapped them. That way, he could get back at Maggie and make five thousand dollars too. So he left her the ransom note, but chickened out in the end."

"I like it!" Frank beamed. "That would tie everything to the smuggling ring. Let's go to police headquarters. We can find out where they're keeping the porpoises. Then we'll call Maggie and have her meet us. She could see if Sam and Samantha are among them."

With high hopes, Frank, Joe, and Fred circled quickly around the lower level toward the exit. It was after five o'clock, and almost everyone else had already gone.

On their way out, Joe glanced briefly through an observation window at the sharks and sting-rays in the main tank. Then he gasped.

"Hey! There's a couple of guys fighting in there!" he cried.

Joining Joe at the window, Frank and Fred looked up toward the surface of the tank. Sure enough, two men were in the water, thrashing wildly at each other. The boys strained to see their faces, but through the tangle of bubbles and bodies it was impossible.

Just then, one of the fighters broke away from the other and began swimming underwater toward the side of the tank. His features were now vaguely visible. He was a young man, and had longish red hair.

Not wasting another second, the three youths rushed to the stairs. It took less than half a minute to get to the upper level, but by the time they did, the fight was over and only one of the men remained. *He was Skip!*

"Who were you fighting in there?" Frank asked the muscular porpoise trainer, who sat on the lip of the tank, soaking wet and coughing up swallowed water.

"None of your business!" Skip growled.

Joe sighted a trail of wet footsteps leading to the back stairs. "He went this way!" the blond boy shouted as he leaped down the stairs in pursuit.

Instead of following his brother, Frank ran to the railing at the edge of the upper level, where there was a clear view of the parking lot. He reached it just in time to witness the red-haired man jump into a blue Chevy van and drive off. A moment later, Joe dashed out into the parking area, followed by Fred.

"He got away!" Frank yelled from the railing. "Stay there, I'll be right down." He descended the back stairs and joined the two in the parking lot.

"The red-haired guy drove off in a blue van," Frank reported. "Probably Skip's."

"What do you think he and Skip were fighting about?" Fred asked.

Frank shrugged. "I don't know."

"What do we do next?" Joe queried.

"Let's go to the police," Frank suggested, looking at his watch. "I'd like to check out those smugglers and the stolen porpoises before it gets dark."

The trio piled into Maggie's pickup and drove south to the city of Melbourne, where the criminals were held by the police. On the way, they discussed Skip and the redheaded man.

"My hunch is that they are partners," Joe said. "Skip handles the inside work and the other guy steals the animals. That would account for Skip's alibis whenever there was a theft. He'd make sure he was somewhere where he'd be seen by plenty of people."

"All we have to do is find out who that redhead is," Frank said.

"Maybe he's one of the smugglers," Fred proposed. "One who wasn't caught."

Joe nodded as he pulled up the pickup in front of the Melbourne police headquarters. Then the three climbed out and entered the building. They found one of the detectives who was working on the case. His name was Robert Barnes.

He was interested in their theory, even though he was not able to allow them to question the smugglers. "But if you'd like to look at the porpoises," Detective Barnes said, "you're welcome to do so. They're in a saltwater swimming pool about a mile from here. And I'd like Fred to go through our files. Maybe he can identify the other man who visited his house."

"May we call Mrs. Russell and ask her to come here?" Frank said. "She'd be able to pick out her pets if they're among the porpoises."

"Certainly."

While Frank called Maggie, Fred pored over several volumes of photographs. By the time Maggie arrived, he had not found anyone that looked familiar.

Officer Barnes gave the Hardys directions to the pool, and the young detectives and Maggie set out in Maggie's car to check the stolen animals while Fred continued going through the mug shots.

When the trio arrived at the pool, they found Mr. Brewster there, who had already picked out four of the porpoises as belonging to Sealand.

The Hardys told him about the fight between Skip and the redhead. "Do you have any idea who this man could be?" Frank asked when he was finished.

"No," Mr. Brewster replied. "No one fitting your description works for Sealand. But I'll keep an eye out for him and will let you know if he shows up again."

"Thanks," Frank said.

Maggie, who had anxiously surveyed the pool while the others were talking, came back and joined the group. Her face was sad.

"Sam and Samantha aren't here," she said. "I had so hoped that—" Her voice broke and she turned away.

"Maybe we had it all wrong," Joe said, discouraged. "Perhaps it was a kidnapping after all and had nothing to do with the Sealand thefts and the smugglers. We have to rethink this whole thing."

The Hardys and Maggie drove back to the police station, where she let them out of her car. "I don't think I need to come in," she said. "I'd rather just go home. See you later."

When Frank and Joe went inside, they found Fred in a small room with a stack of volumes on a table in front of him. He looked up and brushed a strand of hair from his forehead. "How'd you make out?" he asked.

"No luck," Frank said.

"I'm sorry," Fred said. "I was hoping Mrs. Russell would get her pets back. But listen, I have some great news!"

"What is it?" Joe asked eagerly.

Fred pointed to a picture in one of the books. "Here's the other man who came to my house!" he said.

"Wonderful!" Frank exclaimed.

"But that's only the half of it!" Fred said excitedly. "Take a look at this one!" He pointed to another picture.

Frank and Joe crowded around him and stared at the photograph.

"It's the redheaded guy we saw at Sealand!" Frank cried out.

8   A Scream for Help

Although the Hardys had only caught a fleeting glimpse of the man as he swam underwater in the Sealand tank, they clearly recognized his face in the photo.

"This is great news!" Frank said.

Pulling up chairs, the young detectives read the information on both criminals. There was an address for the man who had visited Fred. His name was James "Bags" Bediker and he'd been arrested a few years back for loansharking. The redhead, Jason Meld, had no permanent address. The file indicated that he lived on a houseboat and had a record of petty larceny.

"Let's talk to Detective Barnes," Frank said, and the boys went back into the officer's room.

"That's very interesting," the detective said when he had heard their story. "We don't have anything on these men right now that would warrant their arrest, but if you can prove that they're involved in thefts, we can move right in."

"We'll try," Frank promised.

Barnes nodded. "Let me know how you're progressing and if you need any help."

After saying good-bye, the three boys left headquarters and climbed into the pickup.

"Tomorrow we'll check out Bags Bediker's place and try to locate Jason Meld's house-boat," Frank said.

"Can I come with you?" Fred asked.

"Sure. We'll pick you up in the morning," Joe said.

After dropping Fred off at home, the young detectives went to Maggie's beach house. They found their hostess sitting outside, gazing gloomily at the empty lagoon.

"My pets are still missing, and so is the Aristo satellite," Maggie said sadly. "This wasn't a very successful day."

"Don't worry, we have some new clues,"

Frank said and told her what they had found at headquarters. "We'll get to the bottom of this mystery yet," he promised.

Next morning the Hardys drove inland to pick up Fred. He knew the area and guided them to Bediker's house, which was about ten miles farther west.

"I can't figure out why a loan shark would be interested in electric eels," Fred said. He knew that a loan shark was someone who made a living by lending people money for enormously high interest rates, and, if they could not repay the loan, would often apply brutal force to make them pay.

"That's what we're here to find out," Frank replied as he parked the pickup some distance from the man's tidy one-story house surrounded by palm trees.

The boys hid behind shrubbery near the place. Not long afterward they saw Bediker come out, get into his car, and drive off.

Quickly the young detectives ran to the pickup and followed their suspect. He stopped in front of a run-down apartment house, went inside, and soon emerged with another man.

"Let's see where he's taking this guy," Joe said as he followed the car at a safe distance.

Bediker drove east until he reached a decrepit bungalow on a deserted stretch of beach. There was no sign of life around it, and the boys had to park quite a distance away in order not to be spotted. Then they sneaked up to the bungalow on foot and tried to peek inside, but all the windows were closed and covered by shades.

"What'll we do now?" Joe whispered.

"We'll wait around the side and see what happens," Frank said.

Suddenly, from inside the house came a horrible cry of pain.

"Aaaaaaaaeeeeeeeeee!"

Frank, Joe, and Fred rushed to the front door, which was open. They dashed into the bungalow and found Bags' companion bound to a chair by leather straps. Wires ran from the chair to an induction coil, then into a saltwater aquarium containing an electric eel!

Bediker stood next to the chair, gaping at the unexpected intruders.

"It's a homemade electric chair!" Frank cried out. "Quick, untie that man!"

While Fred hastened to free the hapless victim, Frank and Joe overpowered the loan shark, who had no chance to defend himself.

"You can't do that!" he protested loudly.

"You can't just run into my house without a warrant! Who are you, anyway?"

"Detectives," Frank said shortly. "And we're making a citizen's arrest!"

"Who's pressing charges?" Bags challenged.

"I'm sure this gentleman here would be happy to oblige!" Joe said, pointing to the victim.

"He wouldn't dare!" Bags screamed. "You know what'll happen to you if you do that, don't you, Arthur?"

The man looked bewildered. "No, no," he said after a few moments. "I don't want to press charges."

"What?" Frank stared at him incredulously.

"He's afraid of retribution," Joe said. "Bags probably has other guys working with him."

Bags smirked. "See?"

The boys looked at him in disgust. They could see how he received the name Bags. His clothes were ill-fitting and baggy. His graying hair was combed straight back, and his figure was slight.

"What exactly is going on here?" Frank demanded.

"I tell you what's going on!" Fred exclaimed. "This creep is using my Sparky to give his clients electric shocks. Now I know why he came to my house and wanted to know all about adjusting the current and whatnot. He doesn't want to really hurt them, just cause enough pain to make them pay!"

"And the eel is yours?" Frank asked in surprise.

"That's right!" Fred said gleefully. "It's Sparky!"

"Great!" Joe said. "I'm sure the police will be happy to arrest our friend here for theft. We won't even need anyone else to press charges."

The smug expression dropped from Bags Bediker's face. "I didn't steal that eel," he said. "I bought it before I went to Fred's house to find out how to use it. There's no electricity in this place—"

"Possession of stolen property is still a crime," Frank cut in sharply.

"Suppose I tell you all I know and I give you the eel back," Bags pleaded. "Will you leave the police out of it?"

Frank thought for a moment. Without the support of the loan shark's victim there was not much chance that Bags would be arrested as long as he returned the eel, which he claimed not to have stolen.

"It depends on how much you tell us," the young detective finally said. "And whether you promise not to torture your clients anymore."

"I can't tell you the name of the guy who sold me the eel," Bags said cautiously. "He doesn't let his identity be known to his customers. But I do know that he steals sea animals and sells them at a cut-rate price in the underworld. He supplied those porpoises to the smuggling ring that was just captured."

"We know about them," Joe cut in. "And we know that the man who went with you to Fred's house was caught."

Bags nodded. "He's the one who told me about the supplier and set up the deal. He'd read about Fred in the paper, and after I bought the eel, he took me over there to learn the tricks. I had no idea that the eel actually belonged to Fred."

"I can't believe my Sparky was used to hurt people!" Fred said angrily. "And to think I even told him how to do it!"

Bags shrugged. "I didn't hurt them much. Just enough to remind them that next time they'd better pay up!"

"Not much, eh?" Frank said. He signaled his brother with his eyes, and Joe instantly knew what he was getting at. Both boys grabbed the loan shark at the same time, dragged him across the floor, and threw him down into his own makeshift torture chair.

"What are you doing?" Bags cried as the youths strapped his arms and legs to the chair. "I told you everything I know!"

"We don't believe you," Frank shot back, fastening another of the leather straps. "So we're going to give you a taste of your own medicine."

"Fred, why don't you take the controls?" Joe said when he was done. Out of view of the loan shark, he signaled the boy only to pretend. "You know how to work this contraption. And give Mr. Bediker here a nice big dose."

"Sure!" Fred exclaimed. "I'll be glad to give him a full blast."

Bediker's unfortunate visitor, the man who had not been able to pay his debts, could hardly suppress a grin when Fred walked to the dial and set it up high. The boy made sure Bediker did not notice that he had secretly disconnected one of the wires leading to Sparky's tank, rendering the electric eel harmless.

Seized with terror, Bags Bediker's eyes fixed on Sparky, who swam lazily from one end of the tank to the other. He knew that the eel could put out five hundred volts, enough to stun a man, and that it could continue giving impulses for a long time.

"That's too high!" he sputtered in fear. "That'll hurt me!"

"It won't if you answer our questions before Sparky decides to light up," Frank said. "Now tell us the name of the sea animal supplier and we'll turn off the current."

"Okay!" Bags squeaked, breaking into a cold sweat. "His name is Jason Meld. He lives on a houseboat on the Intracoastal Waterway. Now get me out of here!"

Suddenly, Sparky made a quick turn and the voltage meter jumped all the way up. Bags groaned and slumped back in the chair, shutting his eyes. A few moments later he looked up as if he expected to see a chorus of angels surrounding him. Instead, he saw the grinning faces of Frank, Joe, Fred, and his client, Arthur.

"You tricked me!" he howled, his face turning red with anger. "You scared me for nothing!"

"Would you rather it had been for real?" Joe challenged.

"Why, you!" Bags cried, trying to tear himself free of the leather straps. "You'll pay for this!"

The boys couldn't keep from laughing. Finally Frank controlled himself. "Let's get Sparky and go home," he said. "We can leave Mr. Bediker in his chair. He'll manage to wriggle out of it in a couple of hours."

He adjusted the leather straps to make it easier for the man to escape, then turned to Fred. "How can we transport the eel?"

"The same way the thief brought him over here," Fred said, pointing to a large, watertight plastic bag. It was draped over a grocery cart, which had apparently been used to move the container once it was filled with water.

Soon the boys had filled the bag and put Sparky inside. They rigged up a ramp so they could push the cart right onto the pickup, then offered Bediker's client a ride.

"I . . . I think I'd better stay," Arthur said, obviously fearing retribution from the loan shark if he left him in his present predicament. "But thanks anyway."

Frank nodded and the boys climbed into the cab of the pickup. Driving as carefully as possible, they returned to Fred's house.

"It looks as if the porpoise thief hired Jason Meld to do the dirty work," Joe said on the way. "We'll have to find him and make us tell him who his boss is. It won't be easy."

"It won't even be easy to find Jason," Frank

said with a sigh. "The Intracoastal Waterway runs along the East Coast from Florida to Maine. That's over a thousand miles."

He knew that the waterway, which was built by the Army Corps of Engineers, was a route by which boats could travel along the coast without ever having to enter the open ocean. It covered an immense distance, and thousands of boats used it every year. Locating a houseboat on it could take weeks of constant search.

"I don't think we'll have too much trouble," Joe said. "The waterway runs right past Sealand, and we saw Jason there yesterday. I'll bet his houseboat is nearby."

Frank wasn't listening. He was staring into the rearview mirror, watching a white sedan.

"What's the matter?" Fred asked.

"We're being followed!" Frank declared.

9 Scare on the Road

Joe twisted in his seat to observe the traffic behind them. "Are you sure?" he asked.

"Pretty sure," Frank replied. "It's a white sedan, and it's been with us for some time."

"Then pull over, and let's check it out."

Frank swung the pickup into a side street and stopped. A minute passed; then the white sedan made the same turn. As it did, Frank yanked the steering wheel hard to the left and stepped on the gas. The truck lunged into the middle of the street, broadside to the sedan. With its way blocked, the car screeched to a stop.

All three youths leaped from the pickup and ran toward it. Two men were inside.

Suddenly, the sedan lurched forward!

"Watch out!" Frank yelled, jumping out of the car's path.

The boys leaped aside as the sedan hurtled over the curb and bounced, with tires spinning, up on the sidewalk. Once it was beyond the pickup, it skidded back to the street and sped off.

"Did anyone get a good look at those guys?" Frank asked, peering after the vehicle.

"There was too much reflection in the windshield for me to see their faces," Joe said. "But I did get the license number."

The boys returned to the pickup, where Joe quickly jotted down the number. Then they resumed their trip to Fred's house. Neither Frank nor Joe talked much on the way, but both boys shared the same thought. The men in the sedan had probably been hired by Megavision to get Joe out of the way!

"Well, at least we've lost them for now," Joe sighed. "If we're lucky, they won't find us again for a while." He glanced in the rearview mirror at the water bag. Despite the rough driving, the electric eel seemed to be all right. "Sorry about that," he apologized to Fred. "But it looks as if Sparky's okay."

"Yes," the boy answered anxiously. "But the sooner we get him home, the better."

Once they were at Fred's house, the boys wheeled the eel inside. Then, leaving their friend to take care of his pet, Frank and Joe headed for the Space Center.

There they found Chet and Mr. Hardy with Mr. Stone in the control room. They related the morning's events to them.

"I'll have the police trace that license number," Mr. Hardy said. "It does look as if Megavision is already gunning for our star witness. I want you to be extra careful, Joe."

"I will be, Dad," Joe gulped, handing over the piece of paper with the white sedan's tag number on it.

"Wow! I wish I'd come along," Chet Morton spoke up, amazed at the account of the loan shark and his eel-powered electric chair.

Frank chuckled. "Well, you can help us with what we have to do next. But tell us, is there any news on the missing satellite?"

"Only that we're certain it's not up there," Mr. Hardy replied. "The laser optics telescope confirmed that."

"How about Megavision?" Joe spoke up. "Is there any chance they got to it somehow?"

"They've been very close-mouthed since the sabotage attempt." Mr. Hardy shrugged. "Neither I nor the police have been able to get anything out of them."

"Could they have planted a bomb aboard the satellite before it went up?" Joe queried.

"Nobody but top personnel were allowed near the satellite before the launch," Mr. Stone said. "No unauthorized people would have had the chance. And all functions were A-okay before and during the launch. If the satellite had been tampered with, we would have picked it up on our computers."

"Talking about computers, however," Mr. Hardy said, "I've come up with something interesting. It has to do with your friend, Maggie."

"Maggie?" Joe uttered in disbelief. "What could she have to do with —"

"Just listen," his father interrupted. "This afternoon we discovered that one of the main computers here, the one Maggie was operating, had logged some input that is not part of the launch procedure. The nature of the input is unknown, but we do know that the computer

94

was tampered with, and that it happened within two days before the launch."

"Did you talk to Maggie about this?" Frank asked.

Mr. Hardy nodded. "She says she followed the procedure to the letter and is as mystified by the unknown input as we are. I'm inclined to believe her."

"So someone else must've used the computer while Maggie wasn't there," Joe deduced.

"That's the interesting part," Mr. Hardy went on. "During the two days before the launch, Maggie only left her post twice. Once she went home for the night. The other time was between three and five o'clock on the day she was supposed to meet with the man who kidnapped her porpoises."

Joe whistled as he realized the implication of this.

"Now," Mr. Hardy continued. "At night Space Center security is very tight, and only a few people are permitted inside. But during the day, when Maggie was trying to get her pets back, many people are in the Center with low clearance. One of those could have sneaked into her room and tampered with the computer."

Frank knitted his brow and looked quizzically at his father. "And you think this somehow ties in with the missing satellite?"

"I don't know," Fenton Hardy replied, throwing his hands in the air. "But it sure smells fishy to me."

Just then, Mr. Stone's assistant strode into the control room and spotted the two boys. "There's a phone call for you," he said.

"You can take it at my desk," Mr. Stone offered.

Frank and Joe followed him into his office, and Frank picked up the receiver.

"Hi," Fred's voice came over the line. "Guess what! I found Jason's houseboat!"

10   *Mistaken Identity*

"Great!" Frank exclaimed. "We were about to start looking for Jason Meld ourselves. How'd you find the houseboat so fast?"

"It was easy," the boy replied proudly. "Once I'd set up Sparky in his tank, I drove down toward Sealand. There's a bridge that crosses the Intracoastal Waterway. There I spotted this houseboat tied to a dock. I decided to check it out. After talking to a couple of local people, I learned that a red-haired man lives on it. I figured it had to be Jason."

"What a lucky break!" Frank beamed. "Where are you now?"

"At a phone booth on the far side of the

bridge," Fred answered. "Why don't you meet me here?"

"We will." After taking down directions to the bridge, Frank hung up and related the conversation to his brother.

"So what are we waiting for?" Joe exclaimed, snapping his fingers in delight. "Let's go!"

The Hardys bolted from Mr. Stone's office and returned to the control room to tell their father about the call.

"Get in touch with me if you come up with something," Mr. Hardy said as the boys were walking out the door with Chet. "I'll check on the white sedan's license number in the meantime."

The trio followed Fred's direction to the phone booth near the bridge. When they arrived, the Hardys introduced Chet to their new friend. Then Fred led them down a narrow, sandy road until they reached an old dock. Tied to it was a big, modern houseboat. It was a boxy structure sitting atop a rectangular platform, and was painted a light shade of aquamarine.

"I don't think Jason is home," Fred remarked. "I watched the place for a long time and didn't see anyone."

Frank looked at his wristwatch. "Why don't you and Chet stake out this place for another hour? I want to go with Joe and report that loan shark to the police. We'll be back soon."

"Sure," Fred said. "But take this. It may come in handy." He handed the boys an electronic beeper with which they could signal to another unit that he kept.

"Where'd you get these?" Joe asked.

"I brought them from home. You know I like electronic gadgets."

Joe grinned. "I'm glad you do."

Chet and Fred found hiding places in the bushes near the old dock, while the Hardys took off again in the pickup. They not only wanted to report the episode with Bags, but also hoped Detective Barnes had some new information on how the porpoises had been supplied to the smuggling ring.

But when the youths arrived at headquarters, the detective admitted that he had come up with nothing. The captive smugglers still refused to talk. So, after making their report, Frank and Joe returned to the houseboat.

"Any signs of Jason?" Joe asked when they joined Fred at his hiding place near the dock.

"Not yet," the boy answered.

"What about Chet?" Frank inquired. "Where's he?"

"He went to find a hiding spot on the other

side," Fred replied. "Said he wanted to get a better angle on the houseboat."

"Hey, what's that?" Joe exclaimed suddenly, looking over Fred's shoulder.

All heads turned to the water beyond the dock. Something was moving slowly just below the surface. It looked like a big animal of some kind.

"It's probably a sea cow." Fred laughed.

"A what?" Joe blurted.

"A sea cow," Fred repeated. "They're really called manatees. They like to feed on the vegetation in the waterway, and it's not uncommon to see one out here. They're huge, almost grotesque-looking animals. That's how they got the name sea cow. Often they weigh over a thousand pounds."

Frank whistled. "That big, eh?"

Fred nodded. "It's said that sailors used to mistake manatees for mermaids back in the olden days. But if you saw one, you'd find that hard to believe. They're fat, ugly, lumbering creatures. But they're harmless."

Just then, the sea cow poked its head out of the water and gazed around.

"Hey!" Frank cried. "That's no sea cow—it's Chet!"

Spotting the Hardys on shore, the chubby youth waved and began swimming toward them.

"What's so funny?" he sputtered, finding his friends doubled over with laughter as he climbed out of the water in his undershorts.

"What were you doing in there?" Joe asked.

"I wanted to hide under the bow of the houseboat," Chet replied, "so when Jason came back I could hear everything he said and did. But I got cold waiting."

"That was good thinking," Joe said. "Especially for a sea cow."

"Sea cow?" The chubby youth frowned. "What do you mean?"

"Never mind," Joe chortled. "We'll tell you about it later."

Just then Frank spotted a blue Chevy van drive over the bridge and turn down the sandy road. "Quick!" he cried. "Everyone hide!"

All the boys dashed into the bushes except Chet. Dripping wet as he was, he ran back to the spot where he had left his clothes.

Skip Adkins was driving the van. He pulled up to the dock and let out his passenger—it was Jason Meld! Then he turned around and drove off.

The red-haired houseboat owner watched him leave before he marched down the dock and boarded his craft.

"We could take on that creep right now!" Joe whispered, peering through the bushes.

"No," Frank decided. "If we confront him at this point, we would only give away that we're on to him. Even if we could prove he's the thief, we might never find out what he did with Maggie's pets, or who his boss is. Let's wait and watch for now."

No sooner had Frank spoken than the youths saw a truck pull up to the houseboat. A man stepped out and went inside.

"This may be the guy we're looking for," Frank muttered.

"How about we send Chet in under a pretext," Joe suggested. "These guys have never seen him before and perhaps he could pick up a clue."

Frank nodded. "That sounds like a good idea. Where is he?"

"Somewhere on the far side of the dock, I suppose," Joe replied.

"Then let's send Fred after him. I have a plan."

"What's that?" Joe asked as he signaled Fred, who was hiding nearby.

"We'll have Chet and Fred work the situation from this end while you and I follow the truck."

Fred crawled over from his nearby bush, and Frank, in a hushed voice, told him his strategy.

"Okay," Fred said. "I'll tell Chet. And we'll wait an hour before making our move."

Not wasting another second, Frank and Joe stealthily crept down the sand lane to Maggie's pickup. Then they climbed inside and waited.

"Here he comes," Joe said after ten minutes had passed.

The truck wheeled out onto the main road and turned right, away from the bridge. It was heading inland. The driver was the stranger. Frank and Joe had gotten a good look at him while they had been watching from the bushes. He was short and lean, with a tight-fitting T-shirt and jeans to show off his wiry, suntanned physique. His face was narrow, his lips thin and drawn together in a constant sneer, and his skin was rough.

Frank didn't start the pickup's engine until the truck was some distance ahead of them. Then he pulled out into the traffic and followed.

Trailing the truck wasn't easy. It turned north on a major highway and continued for almost an hour before exiting onto another highway bound for Gainesville, a city in north-central Florida. Then, to the boys' surprise, it skirted the city and headed toward Fantasieworld.

Joe scratched his head in wonder. "What's he going there for?"

Fantasieworld, the boys knew, was a famous children's fairyland of shows, rides, and thrills of all kinds.

"I don't know," Frank mused.

Soon, however, the boys' question was answered as the truck pulled into an "Employees Only" parking lot.

"That guy works here!" Joe exclaimed.

11 Chet Disappears

Frank drove slowly past the employees' entrance and saw the truck disappear down a ramp. Guards were posted there, preventing outsiders from gaining access.

By now, the boys' minds were burning with curiosity. What kind of deal could Jason have made with a Fantasieworld employee?

"Let's check with the officials here and find out who that guy is," Frank said, pulling into a public parking area.

After getting out, the brothers boarded a monorail train that was used to transport visitors into the immense amusement park. On the way, they questioned the operator and were directed to the Fantasieworld personnel manager, Mr. Laker.

"What can I do for you boys?" he asked as the brothers entered his office. He was a jolly, heavyset man wearing a blue suit and a red bow tie.

Frank and Joe told him their suspicions and gave him a description of the man in the truck.

Mr. Laker frowned. "We screen our applicants very carefully before giving them a job," he said. "If this fellow is mixed up in anything illegal, I want to know about it. If he's not, I don't want any rumors being spread about him. It's bad for our image here, you understand."

"We understand," Frank said. "And if you'll help us, we can keep our investigation very quiet. No one has to know who we are or why we're here."

The heavyset man adjusted his bow tie and paused for a moment to think. "I'll have to speak to my superiors before I okay any kind of special clearance for you," he finally spoke. "At this point, I can only give you the man's name and job classification."

Mr. Laker riffled through a set of employee files in his desk drawer and drew out a folder. From a photo, the boys recognized the thin-lipped little man they'd trailed from Jason's houseboat. His name was Buster Randolph, and he was a maintenance man for one of the shows, the Bear Dance. The Hardys also learned that Buster had been employed at Sealand before he had come to Fantasieworld.

"Check with me later," the personnel manager said, closing the folder and returning it to his desk drawer. "I'll see if I can get you special clearance to the employees' area. And take these." He smiled, handing them a booklet of show tickets. "This way you can have some fun while you wait."

Thanking Mr. Laker, the Hardys left his office and headed for the amusements. They wandered past the Outer Space Planet, the Deep Sea Submarine Ride, and a host of other attractions until they reached the Bear Dance.

"Let's go in," Joe said. "Maybe we'll find Buster."

"Oh, you just want to see the show," Frank teased his younger brother. "But I admit, I wouldn't mind seeing it either."

The Hardys handed two tickets to a man at the door and entered the theater. In a few moments, the lights dimmed and the Bear Dance began. It was so delightful that the boys forgot all about Buster for a while. Singing bears danced on stage, playing banjos and guitars.

They were not real, but neither were they actors dressed up in costumes. They were mechanical robots that moved and spoke like people. The audience was thrilled by the show and applauded enthusiastically when it was over.

"That was great!" Joe beamed as they emerged from the theater. "Now let's sample some of the rides."

Frank and Joe encountered the Island Pirates on a boat ride, then had a scary trip through the Haunted House. Both were just as entertaining as the Bear Dance had been, containing a host of lifelike mechanical dummies. Except for ushers and ticket takers, there were no people anywhere!

By the time the boys returned to Mr. Laker's office, they were wondering where all the Fantasieworld employees were hiding!

"That's why I had to get you special clearance," the personnel manager replied to their question, his eyes twinkling at the youths' bafflement. "Most of our staff here operates in a network of underground tunnels. That way, they never spoil the fantasy of it all by being seen by the visitors. Your suspect, Randolph, spends every one of his working hours out of sight."

"What do they do in these tunnels?" Joe queried.

"Run the shows," the jolly man replied. "The mechanical dummies and all the other effects are controlled by an intricate computer system hidden underground. Some of our people are top-notch computer experts, many of whom came to work here after they retired from the NASA space program. The rest perform a variety of jobs, from constructing the shows and maintaining them to sweeping the floors."

An idea formed in Frank's mind at the mention of computers and the space program. "Can we go down in those tunnels and look around?" he asked in an excited tone. "I have a strong suspicion that if Buster is up to something, it has to do with his work here. I'd like to keep an eye on him."

The manager nodded. "I've arranged for you to do just that tomorrow morning. I've checked up on you boys and was happy to learn that you have excellent reputations as amateur detectives. If there's any mischief going on here, I'm certain you'll get to the bottom of it."

Frank smiled. "We'll try."

"But remember," Mr. Laker went on. "Stay undercover and don't ask too many questions. I wouldn't want any nasty rumors floating around about Fantasieworld and our employees."

"We'll be careful," Joe promised, shaking the man's hand. "And we'll be back tomorrow to get to work."

Fred and Chet, meanwhile, had remained in the bushes near Jason's houseboat, preparing to carry out their end of Frank's plan.

No other strangers had arrived after the sleuths' departure, so Chet decided it was time to make their move.

"Okay, this is it," he said as he stepped from the bushes and walked toward the dock.

Fred looked on as Chet marched to the houseboat and knocked on the door, pretending to be interested in buying barracudas.

If the plan worked, they could catch the sea animal thief in the act of plying his trade and force him into disclosing who had hired him for the job. Fred kept his fingers crossed as the door opened and Chet disappeared inside.

Ten minutes passed and Chet did not return. Fred was growing uneasy. "Come on!" he urged under his breath, checking his watch for what seemed the hundredth time. "You've been in there long enough!"

But when another ten minutes had gone by, it was clear that the plan had backfired. Not only did Chet not come out of the houseboat, but its engines started and it slowly pulled away from the dock! Jason himself appeared on deck only once to throw off the bow lines.

"Oh, no!" the thin boy groaned, watching the houseboat motor out into the waterway. "He's taking Chet along as his prisoner!"

12   Rescue Attempt

Fred almost ran out on the dock in pursuit, then decided against it. It was too late for him to get aboard, and the sight of him might jeopardize Chet even more.

But Fred had no intention of letting the aquamarine houseboat just disappear. Staying in the bushes only long enough to see it turn south on the Intracoastal Waterway, he dashed to his car and drove to the center of the bridge, planning to jump from there to the houseboat's roof. But he was too late. By the time he was out of his car, Jason Meld and his prisoner had already passed beneath him.

"Rats!" the skinny youth muttered, seeing

the boat continue down the waterway. He hopped back into his car and drove alongside it. There was another bridge seven miles farther south, he knew.

On the way, though, the boy was beginning to have doubts about his heroic plan. He realized it was a dangerous and foolish move. He'd probably end up breaking a leg—or worse.

Thinking more clearly now, Fred reviewed the situation. He began to wonder whether Chet had been kidnapped at all. Maybe Jason was simply taking him to a stash of stolen animals to show him barracudas. All Fred had to do was to follow the houseboat to its destination!

He clutched the wheel of his car even tighter and continued down the coast road until another thought occurred to him. Chet would never have gone off alone with Jason unless he had been forced into it. I was right the first time, Fred told himself gloomily. Chet must have been kidnapped. I have to stop that boat!

From the coastal road, the waterway wasn't visible, but Fred knew he was traveling faster than Jason's houseboat. He would be able to intercept it at the next bridge. It was rush hour, however, and soon traffic began to slow. It would be close!

He still had no idea how to stop Jason other than to jump on the houseboat's roof and try taking on the thief all by himself. But when he came closer, he remembered that the bridge was a drawbridge. If he could prevent if from opening, he'd have Jason trapped!

Grinning, he drove onto the span and halted right in the middle, where the bridge separates. However, as soon as he stopped he began to block traffic, and a long line of cars piled up behind him.

Horns began to honk and angry voices could be heard. Fred looked down in the water. As he had expected, the aquamarine houseboat was chugging along toward the bridge, no more than a hundred yards away.

"Hey, buddy!" a man yelled behind him. "Move your car! This isn't a rest stop, you know!"

Fred saw the man shaking a fist out his window. The chorus of horns became louder and louder. Since he had prevented the bridge from opening, boat horns were soon joining in and people were getting angrier by the minute.

Just then, the drawbridge operator marched from his booth toward Fred. He was big, and he looked mad. "What's the idea?" he shouted above the din of honking cars and boats.

"You're blocking all the traffic! Are you out of your mind?"

"I . . . I have to stop one of those boats," Fred pleaded. "A friend of mine is being held captive, and I can't let the boat go through. You have to—"

"I have to open this bridge!" the operator snapped angrily. "Now move this instant or I'll call the police!"

Fred hesitated. Maybe he *should* let the drawbridge operator call the police. He could tell them his story and have Jason arrested. He glanced at the houseboat, which was waiting with a collection of other craft for the bridge to open. But Fred realized that if the police would not listen to him before making him move his car and detain him for creating a disturbance, he would lose Chet and the houseboat for good.

"I said move it!" the angry operator repeated. "Don't you understand English?"

Without another word, Fred drove from the bridge. On the other side, he pulled off the road and watched as the span opened and the boats went through. Then, before the long line of angry commuters was allowed to continue, Fred swung back into the traffic. He turned south again on the road that followed the waterway on the opposite side.

For the next hour, he zigzagged back and forth over bridges, keeping tabs on Jason. The bright afternoon sun was sinking quickly in the sky. If Jason didn't stop the boat before it was dark, Fred would lose sight of it and Chet would disappear!

Frank and Joe were still at Fantasieworld. They waited in their pickup at the employees' parking garage. The gigantic amusement park was closing down for the night, and soon Buster Randolph's truck would emerge as people left to go home.

"Here it comes," Joe said, spotting the vehicle.

Again following at a safe distance, they trailed Buster to a bungalow in Gainesville. There, the boys watched him greet a woman and a small child at the front door. Then he went inside and soon the young detectives could see him through the window as he sat down to dinner with his family.

"He doesn't seem like the criminal type to me," Joe sighed, a little embarrassed over their spying.

"Maybe he isn't," Frank agreed. "But looks can be deceiving." He checked his watch. "We should be getting back to Fred and Chet. We'll have plenty of time to investigate Buster tomorrow."

It was a long drive to where the sleuths had left their friends earlier that day. When they finally arrived at the dock, they were surprised to find both the houseboat and their buddies gone!

They ran to the pay phone near the bridge and called first the Space Center, then Fred's house, then Maggie. But nobody had seen or heard from the two boys.

"What happened to them?" Joe cried anxiously, fearing the worst. "They would have called somebody to let us know where they are if they'd had a chance!"

Frank and Joe hurried down to the dock and looked for signs of foul play. But it was now quite dark and they found nothing in the dim moonlight.

"Let's not get too excited about this," Frank said, trying to stay calm. "I'm sure there's an explanation for—"

Suddenly, the electronic beeper in his pocket started to emit a faint signal!

13   Outwitted by a Crook

"It's them!" Joe burst out with glee. "They're trying to signal us!"

Frank pulled the beeper from his pocket and pressed it to his ear to hear better. The beeps were faint, indicating that they were being sent from quite a distance away, and they were coming in a measured sequence. Three beeps. Then a pause. Then six beeps and another pause. Then four beeps.

At first, Frank thought it was Morse code, which he had taught Chet the year before. But after listening to the signal repeat itself several times, it became clear that it wasn't Morse code at all.

A smile appeared on Frank's face. "Get a pad

and pencil out," he told his brother. "I think they're sending us a phone number."

Frank counted the series of beeps as they were transmitted, and Joe jotted them down on the pad. Then Frank answered by sending out several beeps of his own. When he was finished, the Hardys went to the phone booth and dialed the number. It worked!

"I'm so glad to hear from you!" Fred's excited voice came over the line. "I was going to call the Space Center, but I thought I'd try this first."

"Where *are* you?" Frank asked. "And what happened to Jason?"

Fred quickly explained how Chet had been taken hostage aboard the houseboat, and how he had spent the afternoon following it south along the waterway. "I'm at a restaurant right now," he concluded, "a few miles north of Stuart. You should come down here pronto!"

"Do you know where the houseboat is?" Frank inquired.

"Yes," Fred replied tersely. "It seems to have stopped for the night close by."

Pulling out his pad again, Joe wrote down the directions to the restaurant. "Stay there," he said into the mouthpiece before Frank hung up. "We'll join you as fast as we can."

"Boy," Frank said, "my brilliant plan sure

backfired. "Now we not only have to find Maggie's porpoises, but Chet, too!"

"Bags must have called Jason and warned him that a couple of kids were after him," Joe deduced. "So when Chet walked into the houseboat, Jason probably guessed what was up."

It took the better part of an hour for the Hardys to reach the restaurant where Fred was waiting.

He met Frank and Joe outside and climbed into the pickup. Then he directed them to a run-down marina, which was mostly occupied by old fishing boats and shrimp trawlers. The only pleasure craft was the houseboat, tied to the end of one of the docks. Lights were on inside.

Except for a group of palm trees lit up in a tacky display of orange and blue lights, the marina was dark. The three boys crept noiselessly around the trees and onto the dock.

They approached the houseboat and found the door open. Together, they burst inside.

"What the—" Jason yelled, jumping up from a table covered with food wrappers. There was no sign of Chet.

"What did you do with our friend?" Frank demanded hotly of the red-haired man.

"With who?" Jason spat back. He eased from

the table and snatched a spear gun from a wall fitting. "Don't come one step closer!"

The youths moved back a little as they saw the spear gun leveled at them. But they stood their ground.

"Don't play games with us," Joe replied. "A friend of ours visited your houseboat today and he never came out. We have a witness to prove it."

A sly smile appeared on Jason Meld's face. "There's nobody on this boat but me. Go ahead, take a look around and see for yourselves. Don't try anything smart, though, or one of you will wind up with a spear through his belly. I'm not afraid to use this thing, and I'm a very good shot."

The boys didn't doubt it. They slowly backed off and made a thorough search of the boat. But Chet was not there!

"Just because you don't have him aboard doesn't mean you aren't keeping him somewhere else," Frank said to the thief. "We have enough on you to put you in jail right now, if we want."

Jason's smile grew even broader. "That would be a very stupid idea," he said, pointing the spear gun directly at the boy's chest. "If I do have your friend tied up somewhere, and I'm not saying I do, you just may end up taking him home in a wooden box. Understand?"

Frank and Joe realized that Jason was desperate enough to carry out his threat if he had to. But he felt that as long as he had Chet, the boys wouldn't dare go to the police.

"Okay," Fred spoke up. "Give us our friend back and tell us who hired you to steal Maggie Russell's porpoises, and we'll forget the whole thing. Is it a deal?"

"I don't know what you're talking about," the thief lied with a laugh. "Now get out of here."

The three youths had no choice but to back out of the houseboat's door.

"I wonder what happened to Chet," Fed said on the way to their pickup. "I followed that houseboat all afternoon. Jason must have made a quick stop somewhere between bridges to dump Chet."

"I hope he didn't throw him in the water," Frank said tensely.

"What'll we do?" Joe asked.

"Follow Jason's every move," Frank replied.

"I can do that," Fred volunteered. "I've done a pretty good job so far."

"Okay," Frank agreed. "But it's important that Jason doesn't know he's being tailed. Stay out of his sight."

"And call the Space Center as soon as you find out something," Joe added. "Either we'll be there or Dad will take a message for us."

They drove back to the restaurant, where Fred got his car and returned to the marina to keep an eye on the houseboat. Frank and Joe drove to the Space Center to go over things with their father. Even though it was late, the detective was still there.

"Chet's been in tight spots before," Fenton Hardy assured his sons upon hearing the news of the abduction. "He'll be all right."

"We hope so," Joe sighed.

"What about the missing satellite?" Frank said, changing the subject. "Is there any more news on that?"

"Yes, there is. And I also checked the license number on the white sedan that tailed you. It was a rented car, and both the name of the man who rented it and the credit card he used to pay for it were phony."

"That's a bad break," Frank muttered. "But what about the satellite?"

"I've been working on that with Maggie," Mr. Hardy replied. "Come on. She can explain it better than I can."

Frank and Joe followed their father out of the control room and down a hallway. They found the pretty technician in her isolated work area. She looked up expectantly at Frank and Joe as they entered. "Do you have any new leads on Sam and Samantha?" she asked.

Frank winced. He didn't want to worry her with Chet's misfortune or the fact that the man who stole her pets was a very crafty and dangerous criminal. "We think we know who did it," he told her. "And we're hot on his trail. We've already recovered Fred's electric eel."

"Good." Maggie smiled. "I wish we were doing that well with the missing satellite."

Turning back to her computer, she proceeded to show the boys what she and Mr. Hardy had been working on. "We ran tests to see how the computer might've been tampered with and for what reason," she said. "It looks as if someone reprogrammed it before the launch, someone who knew how to operate it very well."

"I still don't see how this could relate to the satellite," Frank queried. "Supposedly the launch was perfect, and the satellite didn't turn up missing until it was in orbit."

"Well, this computer monitored the satellite's functions before and during the launch," Maggie replied. "It could have been reprogrammed to report the sort of test we do on prelaunch simulations. If such a program had interfaced with a satellite emulator, it would have given the impression that we had a real satellite on the rocket."

"What's an emulator?" Joe asked.

"A little electronic box with wires coming out of it. It contains a computer program on a microchip or tape, and poses as the real thing."

"If that's the case, the person who did it must have been both an expert programmer and an expert on satellites and space technology," Frank deduced.

Maggie nodded.

14   A Clever Disguise

"What!" Frank was flabbergasted. "You mean, you may have blasted a multi-million dollar rocket into space with no satellite aboard?"

"It's possible," Maggie said.

Mr. Hardy nodded. "I'll be questioning all the computer technicians tomorrow. I believe it was an inside job."

Frank and Joe were convinced that the theft of Maggie's pets was tied in with the missing satellite. They also felt that the key to the mystery lay somewhere among the maze of tunnels and computers below Fantasieworld.

"I want to go to Fantasieworld as soon as it opens up in the morning," Frank said when they left the Space Center. "Now let's check up on Fred, then hit the hay."

It was late in the evening by the time the Hardys joined Fred in a palm grove near Jason's houseboat. They brought him some food and a sleeping bag they had picked up from Maggie's house. There had been no sign of Chet, and the houseboat's lights were switched off.

"Jason won't go anywhere tonight," Fred remarked, gazing out on the dark marina. "But I bet he'll be on his way early in the morning. I just hope I'll be able to follow him."

"So do we," Frank said.

The Hardys left Fred and drove to Maggie's house. There they went directly to bed. At the crack of dawn they were up and ready to continue their investigation. Before they set out, Frank had an idea.

"Let's take that motorcycle along," he suggested. "This way we can split up if necessary."

"Good idea," Joe said and wheeled the Honda out of the garage. The boys put it in back of the pickup, then drove to Fantasieworld.

When they arrived, they first went to the personnel manager's office.

"I cannot let you be seen in the underground

128

facilities without a cover," Mr. Laker told them. "Otherwise I'd have to explain what you're doing there."

Frank grinned at the jolly man, who today was wearing a canary yellow suit with a green bow tie. "We were talking about that on the way here and came up with a good idea."

From their visit to Fantasieworld the day before, the youths remembered seeing well-known cartoon characters wandering about the amusement park. Unlike the mechanical dummies in the shows, they were real people dressed in costumes, who mingled with the crowds of visitors. To Frank and Joe, this seemed the perfect disguise. Costumed, they could move about unrecognized.

"Excellent!" Mr. Laker agreed. "Let me see if I can get a couple of outfits for you."

The personnel manager picked up his phone and dialed a number. After a minute of talking, he cupped his hands over the receiver and looked at the Hardys. "They have a Dandy Duck, a Silly Milly, and a Piggy Bank costume."

"I'll take Dandy Duck!" Joe announced with a chuckle.

Frank thought for a moment, then said, "I'd like to be Piggy Bank."

"You got 'em!" Mr. Laker beamed.

After relating their requests into the phone, he sent the boys to the costume department, where they were outfitted. Then they returned to Mr. Laker's office for further instructions.

Joe was now Dandy Duck, a big yellow duck in a black suit and ruffled shirt. Frank was dressed up in a pink pig outfit with a slot in his cardboard head.

Mr. Laker laughed. "You look great!" he said. "Now, I'll draw a map of the tunnels for you so you'll find Buster."

When he had finished, he directed Frank and Joe to a stairway leading underground. Soon the young detectives were beneath the complex, walking through a maze of brightly lighted corridors. Disguised as they were, they passed unnoticed as they followed the directions to the Bear Dance. The underground world of the employees bustled with activity. Workers hurried in and out of rooms and were busily engaged in directing the amusements above.

Many nodded greetings to the two cartoon characters as they went by, but luckily no one stopped to chat. The only sticky moment was when another group of costumed characters— Big Bear, Mad Mouse, and Tricky Tom— appeared and tried to talk Frank and Joe into taking a morning coffee break with them. The sleuths mumbled an excuse about being late for a show, then marched off in another direction. When they finally arrived at the section of rooms below the Bear Dance, they looked around for the thin-lipped little man who had visited Jason's houseboat the day before.

"There he is," Frank whispered, spotting him. Buster was having coffee with other maintenance men, who were clustered around a jumble of complicated machinery.

"Let's get a bit closer," Joe suggested.

Concealed within their outfits, the Hardys went to the coffee machine and pretended to be taking a break from work. The men did not pay any attention to them. Intently Frank and Joe listened to their conversation while slowly fixing two cups of tea. But once they made the tea, they were unable to drink it with their disguises on!

"Hey, do you guys want some help with those masks?" one of the maintenance men asked.

"No, no thanks," Frank muttered "We weren't going to drink these. They're for someone else."

"All right." The man grinned, then resumed his conversation with Buster and the others.

The brothers continued to eavesdrop while filling their cups with lemon, milk, and sugar. However, the men were just idly chatting about their jobs, and mentioned nothing suspicious. When they started giving the boys curious glances, Frank and Joe walked away, tea cups in hand.

"What do we do now?" Joe asked, tossing his hot tea into a trash receptacle and leaning against a wall. "This outfit is getting hot and heavy."

The costumes *were* heavy, and the thick material they were constructed of made them stifling hot to wear. Beneath their funny masks, Frank and Joe were starting to perspire.

"Let's hang on as long as we can," Frank said. "Something's going on down here. I can feel it."

For the next few hours, the boys lingered in the corridors around the Bear Dance's subterranean operations area. The poked their heads through open doors, seeing employees at work behind strange and complex machinery. The rooms that housed the large computers, however, were closed, and the Hardys didn't dare go inside for fear they'd be questioned and discovered. Finally they returned to the spot where Buster had taken his coffee break. The men had all disappeared. Too hot and tired to go on, Frank and Joe found an exit to the outside.

"Well, *that* wasn't very successful." Joe shrugged once they were back among the crowds of children in the amusement park.

"I'm still convinced Buster is up to something down there," Frank asserted. "If we could just stick around long enough, I bet we could figure out what it is."

Suddenly, the brothers were surrounded by a group of youngsters. It was a kindergarten class with their teacher, who insisted on having their pictures taken with Piggy Bank and Dandy Duck. Although hot and tired, the two boys obliged, posing with their arms around the children. The little visitors squealed with glee as they hugged Frank and Joe and tugged on their costumes. After the time it was all over, the Hardys trudged back to Mr. Laker's office, perspiring and tired.

"How did you make out?" the manager asked, helping them out of their masks.

Frank wiped the sweat from his dripping forehead. "Nothing so far," he admitted. "But I'm going back down as soon as I've cooled off. First, I'd like to phone my dad, though, if I may."

It was well into the afternoon, and he was anxious to call the Space Center to see if their father had heard from Fred. Using the office phone, he made contact with Mr. Hardy, who informed him that Fred had indeed called an hour earlier and was eager for the sleuths to meet him at a new spot. Fenton Hardy relayed the directions, which Frank wrote on a piece of paper. Then he thanked his father and hung up.

"It's time for us to split up," he told Joe, handing over the directions. "Fred needs help. I'd like to stay here. So would you take the motorcycle to meet him?"

"I'm on my way," Joe agreed and began to pull himself out of his costume.

He left Fantasieworld a few moments later and rode the monorail to the parking lot. Then he took the motorcycle from the back of the pickup and tried to get it started. It took some doing, since it had not been driven in two years, and by the time Joe was on his way, it was beginning to get dark.

From Fred's directions, it was evident that the houseboat was now farther south on the waterway. Getting there from Fantasieworld would take at least two hours. Joe sighed, since he was rather exhausted from wearing the Dandy Duck costume.

He followed the main road from Gainesville. Initially, the wind in his face and the whine of the Honda's engine kept him alert. But after a while, he was becoming a bit drowsy and barely noticed a white sedan pulling up next to him on the highway. Suddenly it made a sharp and sudden swerve.

Crash!

Joe felt a violent pain in his left leg. The wheels of his cycle shot out from under him, and a split second later he and the Honda were hurtling headlong toward a deep ditch on the highway's shoulder!

In the brief instant before he landed, Joe caught a glimpse of the white sedan as it sped away. Then he hit the ground with a thud!

15 Narrow Escape

Joe's shoulder hit first. Then he flipped over and landed flat on his back. He lost consciousness for a few seconds, before his eyes flickered open again. He was badly shaken and felt a dull, thumping pain in his left leg and shoulder. But he was fairly sure nothing was broken.

After a few minutes, he groggily got to his feet. The Honda lay in the ditch a short distance away. Its front wheel had come off the chassis and its frame was bent below the handle bars.

Joe muttered to himself as he climbed out of the ditch. "Well, Megavision, the star witness against you is still alive. Just wait until I get you guys in court!"

No houses or stores lined the barren stretch of highway where Joe had crashed, so he sat down on the side of the road and waited for the police to cruise by. He had no intention of flagging down a car, for fear it could be the crooks coming back to see if the job had been finished. While he waited, he obscured himself within the tall grass bordering the road.

Soon a police patrol did appear. Joe stood up and waved. The squad car, bearing the insignia of the Florida State Police, pulled over and two uniformed officers stepped out.

"You're lucky you weren't killed," one of them said after Joe had described his accident. "I want you to come to headquarters with us and file a report on that white sedan. You can leave your motorcycle here for the time being."

The officer who spoke was a sturdy, rugged man with a high forehead and weathered complexion. His colleague was young, his hair curly and rather long.

"Thanks," Joe said, sliding into the backseat of the patrol car. He was anxious not only to report the sedan, but to call his father and brother.

His relief, however, was short-lived. Instead of getting into the front seat with his partner, the young officer climbed in back. Before Joe

137

had time to react, the man twisted his arm behind his back and slapped a pair of handcuffs on the Hardy boy!

"Hey! What are you doing?" Joe protested, helplessly struggling to free himself. But he had already recognized the awful truth and his face paled. The men weren't police officers at all!

"Shut up!" the phony young officer sneered, pinning his victim to the seat. "Or we'll take care of you right now!"

"You were hired by Megavision, weren't you?" Joe blurted without heeding the warning. "You were the men in the white sedan!"

His answer was a fist landing squarely on his lip, bringing a trickle of blood to the corner of his mouth. He slumped back in his seat and fell silent. But his mind was racing.

Apparently the hired attackers had been following the young detectives to Fantasieworld. Then, when Joe set out on the motorcycle alone, they had taken the opportunity to finish him off. After they had run him down in the white sedan, they had come back in the phony police car to check on their job. Finding Joe alive, they now needed another scheme to dispose of him.

Joe felt the miniature electronic beeper in his pants pocket, but with his arms handcuffed behind his back, it was difficult to reach and nearly impossible to operate. Even if he could send out a signal, he had no idea where he was being taken, so no one could come to his rescue. Things looked bleak.

After a few minutes, the older thug turned down a winding country road. Although the two men didn't allow Joe to speak, they talked to each other, and the boy gathered that they were taking him to one of the huge orange groves that were common to Florida's inland agriculture. A body disposed of in such a vast, uninhabited orchard would never be discovered. Joe groaned at the thought. Out of the window, he could already see long rows of orange trees extending into dark fields on either side of the road.

He also detected something else in his captors' discussion. The younger man was clearly nervous. He was apparently a less experienced hoodlum, and was afraid of being caught. But the weathered, older criminal seemed as cold as stone over what they were going to do. He assured his partner that they would get away with their evil scheme.

The car slowed down, then swung into a narrow dirt road leading into the orange grove. They bounced along in the dark for what seemed about a mile, until they were in the heart of the deserted orchard.

"This is far enough," the older thug grunted, and stopped.

Joe was dragged from the car and tied to a tree. Then the men opened the trunk and drew out two shovels.

"Wha-what are you going to do?" Joe gasped in horror, as the thugs chose a spot and started to dig.

"We're going to bury you," the older man hissed with a nasty gleam in his eye. "Alive!"

Perspiration dripped from Joe's face, which by now was pale with fear. He wrestled to free himself, but it was hopeless. All he managed to free were some oranges that plopped to the ground. One bounced off his head.

"This just isn't your day, is it?" The younger thug chuckled drily, then tossed off his phony police cap and continued digging.

The Hardy boy looked on in terror as dirt flew into the air and the hole grew deeper. But just as the grave was nearing completion, the flames of a small fire appeared about a hundred yards away among the orange trees! A few sec-

onds later, another fire was lighted. Then another.

"What's going on?" the younger man muttered, peering nervously through the trees.

"I'll take a look," his partner replied. "You stay here and watch the kid. If he screams, let him have it with your shovel."

Joe felt his heart leap. He had no idea what the fires were for, either, but perhaps they would save his life! He waited for the older man to disappear among the trees, then cried out, "They found me!" He pretended to be overjoyed at the sight of the fires. "I knew they would come. I knew they'd find me!"

"Shut up!" his captor snapped. Then he glanced toward the mysterious flames in the distance. A fourth fire was now visible. It made him even more nervous. After a moment's pause, he turned back to Joe. "What do you mean?" he growled. "Who found you?"

"The search party," Joe replied gleefully. "Those fires are their torches. They'll be here any minute!"

Again, the man looked from Joe to the distant flames, then back again. "You're lying," he spat, covering up his anxiety with a tough manner. "Nobody knows where you are. It's impossible."

"It's not impossible at all," the blond youth argued. "Take a look in my pants pocket. That will convince you."

The thug reached into Joe's pocket and pulled out the electronic beeper. "What is this thing?" he demanded, eyeing the beeper suspiciously. "Some kind of radio?"

"It's an electronic homing device," Joe answered. "Haven't you ever seen one before? It gives off a beeping signal for miles around, which the police pick up on special radar instruments. They can tell the exact point it's being sent from. I turned the beeper on right after you put me in your car, and now the police are closing in on this spot. You'd better get away fast, or you'll be nabbed for attempted murder. I'll bet they've already arrested your partner."

To Joe's relief, the young thug seemed to fall for the story. He threw the electronic beeper to the ground and tried to crush it with his foot. At that moment, it started to beep.

"Oh, no!" he cried, panicking at the sound. He desperately continued stomping the device until the beeping stopped and the instrument was crushed into the soil.

"That won't do you any good," Joe said slyly. "The police already have this spot pegged.

Look, the torches are getting closer!"

The distant flames had not moved, but the man was so frightened at this point that he believed Joe. Without his partner to reassure him, he did not know what to do.

He broke out in a cold sweat, looking wildly about as if expecting armies of policemen to descend on him at any second. Then, with his hands shaking, he fumbled for the keys to Joe's handcuffs.

"I'm taking you hostage. They can't do anything to me as long as I have you!" he muttered.

Just then, a man walked toward them through the grove. Joe assumed he was the other thug, returning from investigating the fires, and his heart fell. This was it. Now he'd be buried alive for sure!

But the young thug was so scared that he thought it was the police. Quickly he unlocked Joe's handcuffs and began dragging the boy away toward the car. "Don't come any closer or I'll kill him!" he cried toward the dark figure.

"Wait!" his accomplice shouted. "What do you think you're doing? Everything is fine! It was just some smudge fires!"

Recognizing his partner, the man stopped dead in his tracks. He realized that Joe had been fooling him all along, and his face contorted into an angry snarl.

At the same instant, Joe broke free of the would-be killer's grip and bolted into the night!

16   A Clue in the Tunnel

Joe ran as fast as his legs would carry him, dodging between the rows of orange trees. At first the two criminals were close behind him, but eventually he managed to get away in the darkness.

"Phew!" the young detective muttered to himself when he finally leaned against a tree in a state of total exhaustion. "That was too close for comfort."

Once he'd caught his breath, he continued through the immense orange grove at a cautious walk. He had been very lucky so far and did not want to inadvertently run into his captors again. Apparently, the distant flames were indeed

146

smudge fires. During the winter, Joe knew, such fires kept the oranges from freezing during cold spells. "A group of kids must've decided to light up a few," he said to himself. "They probably wanted to have a little fun, but they ended up saving my life!"

After trudging through the orange trees for nearly a mile, he noticed the lights of a small farmhouse. He walked up to it and knocked on the door. A man came out and greeted him.

"May I use your phone?" Joe panted. "It's an emergency."

The man, who said he was the caretaker for the orange grove, looked at him and hesitated. Joe's shirt was ripped from his motorcycle crash, his shoes and jeans were muddy from his escape through the grove, and his mouth was still bloody from his captor's fist.

"Who did you fight with?" the man asked suspiciously.

"Two guys who ran me down on the road, then forced me into their car and brought me here," Joe said and told what had happened.

"So you're one of the Hardy boys, eh?" the man said, still not quite believing the story.

"Yes. You can check with Detective Robert Barnes from the Melbourne police. He knows we're working on recovering two stolen por-

147

poises that belong to Mrs. Maggie Russell."

"Just a minute," the man said and disappeared into his house. A few minutes later he let Joe in. "I called the detective," he admitted. "I wanted to make sure you're really the person you say you are."

"I don't blame you," Joe said. "I guess I do look like a hoodlum."

The man grinned. "There's the phone."

Joe called his father. After hearing his son's story, Mr. Hardy said, "I want you to report to the police right away."

"I will," Joe said. "Did you hear from Fred?"

"Yes. He lost the houseboat. He hasn't seen any sign of Chet, either."

"Oh, no!" Joe groaned. He'd been afraid that Fred might lose track of Jason's boat. Now they might never find Chet again!

"Don't worry," Mr. Hardy said, trying to reassure his son. "I've come up with a plan. Ask if you can spend the night at the caretaker's house and if there's an airfield for small planes nearby."

Joe cupped his hand over the receiver and spoke to his host. Both the caretaker and his wife, who had joined them, told him that they would be happy to put him up, and that, indeed, there was an airstrip nearby. It was used by the orange growers, who had small airplanes for spraying insecticides on the trees.

The young detective thanked the couple for their offer, then related the news to his father.

"Good," Fenton Hardy said. "I've arranged with the Space Center to use one of their planes and pilots tomorrow to help you search for that houseboat. It should be much easier from the air. Fred is coming back here tonight and will be along."

"Thanks, Dad," the boy said. "That's a great idea!" Then he paused. "What about Maggie's motorcycle? It's still on the highway."

"Frank will be going back to Fantasieworld in the morning. He can pick it up."

After giving his father directions to the airstrip and describing where he had left the Honda, Joe hung up. Then he called the police.

In half an hour, a lieutenant arrived and took down the story about the two hired killers. Then Joe took the officer to the place where the men had tied him to the orange tree. The almost finished grave bore out his report, even though the thugs and their car were gone.

When the police report was completed, the officer left and Joe returned to the farmhouse, where he curled up on the sofa.

In the morning, he thanked the caretaker

and his wife for their hospitality and the kindly man drove him to the airstrip. The plane was already there. Joe climbed into the cockpit and sat down next to Fred.

"I hear you had a rough night," Fred said as they taxied out. "I'm glad to see you're still with us."

Joe's body ached, but the caretaker's wife had washed and sewn his clothes, so he was looking much better. "I'm glad, too," he said. "Now all we have to do is find Chet."

The twin engine Scout left the ground and soared toward the clouds. Its pilot was a handsome, square-jawed man named Randy. "Okay, boys," he said. "Where to?"

"South down the waterway," Joe replied. "And keep her low. I don't want to miss the boat."

The pilot maneuvered the craft toward the coast. Soon, the waterway came into view and Randy cut his altitude to a few hundred feet.

While Joe and Fred were searching for Jason Meld, Frank picked up the wrecked Honda, then drove to Fantasieworld, where he went to Mr. Laker's office. He put his Piggy Bank costume on again, then made his way to the underground tunnels, hoping his search would be more fruitful this time.

Soon he found Buster, who was standing at a door to one of the computer rooms, conversing with a white-haired man with glasses inside. The sign overhead read BEAR DANCE. As Frank waddled by, Buster stopped talking and waited until Piggy Bank was well out of earshot.

Frank knew something was up. He walked on until he had turned the corner to an adjoining corridor. There he waited for a few moments before retracing his steps to the computer room. Buster had vanished.

Frank couldn't tell whether the man had entered the room or had gone elsewhere. But he knew he had to take a look inside. Holding his breath, he knocked on the door.

"Who is it?" a voice called out.

Without answering, Frank opened the door and stuck his head inside. The room was full of sophisticated computers, reminding the young detective of Maggie's room at the Space Center. Buster was not there. The white-haired man with glasses sat behind a control panel and looked curiously at his visitor.

"Excuse me," Frank said. "I thought this was the dressing room. I'm new here."

The man laughed. "You must've made the wrong turn somewhere. The dressing room is down the end of corridor twenty-seven."

"Thanks," Frank replied. But instead of leaving, he stepped inside and looked around. "This stuff is amazing," he went on. "I've never seen equipment like this before."

The white-haired programmer leaned back in his chair and sighed. "Oh, it's not so amazing," he said. "I've been working with computers for years."

"I still think it's fantastic," Frank stalled. "I heared that some of you people used to work for NASA."

The programmer chuckled. "Some of us did. I'm not one of them, though. I used to work at a place called Super Tech. It's in Houston, Texas."

"Is this computer like the ones they use in the space program?" Frank asked, still feigning curiosity at the equipment.

"It's similar," the man replied. Then his face soured. "Now, if you'll excuse me, I have lots of work to do. The dressing room is at the end of corridor twenty-seven."

Frank decided not to press his luck. If the computer programmer became suspicious, he might check up on Piggy Bank, and that could mean trouble. The young detective thanked the white-haired man and closed the door. Then he hurried back to Mr. Laker's office.

"Did you come up with any leads?" the personnel manager inquired.

"I think so," Frank told him, stripping off his mask. "May I use your phone? And I'd like to see the file on one of your employees. He has white hair, looks like he's in his late fifties or early sixties, wears glasses, and is one of the people working for the Bear Dance."

While Mr. Laker went through his files, Frank called his father at the Space Center. "I might have something, Dad," he said. "Do you know anything about a company in Houston called Super Tech?"

"Certainly," Mr. Hardy replied. "Super Tech built the Aristo satellite!"

17 *Aerial Search*

"That figures!" Frank exclaimed, snapping his fingers.

"Tell me about it," his father urged.

"A former employee of Super Tech now works on one of the Fantasieland computers," Frank replied.

Mr. Hardy whistled. "You may have hit something."

"Yes," Frank said as he took a file Mr. Laker handed him and opened it. "His name is Larry Web," he went on. "He spent three years at Super Tech before joining Fantasieworld. Do you know what I think? Web may have concocted the phony program for the Space Center computer. It looks like he has the equipment and the know-how."

"What made you suspicious of him?" Mr. Hardy inquired.

"I saw him talking to Buster. They stopped when I walked by. So I checked up on him. I think Buster's job was to get Maggie away from her computer long enough to input the phony program. To do this, he hired Jason to steal her porpoises and send her the ransom note."

"Sounds good," Fenton Hardy said thoughtfully. "But there still are a couple of problems. Even if Mr. Web *did* make up the fake program, and if Buster *did* hire Jason to kidnap Maggie's porpoises to make her leave her post, it doesn't explain how they got into the Space Center and to the computer. There had to be a third partner to do that, someone who was authorized to be at the Space Center and knew how to feed the phony program to the computer."

"What about Doug Davies?" Frank suggested. "He's the satellite's designer and he was at the Space Center the same day that Maggie's computer was tampered with."

"True," Mr. Hardy replied. "And he *is* one of the head people at Super Tech."

"And he probably knew Larry Web before Web switched jobs," the dark-haired boy

155

added. "They could be old friends."

"It wouldn't surprise me if they were," Mr. Hardy agreed. "Megavision could have paid off Davies to sabotage the satellite he built for Aristo. If they launch a bird of their own soon, they'll get all of Aristo's customers. I understand most of them were cable television companies, who cannot wait until Aristo develops a new satellite. They'll cancel their contracts and obtain broadcast transponders on Megavision's satellite."

Frank nodded. "That makes sense. Of course, the villain doesn't have to be Davies. Megavision could have pressured one of the Space Center technicians into making the program switch."

"Possibly Maggie," his father said grimly. "I know it's hard to believe, but even the sweetest people do strange things if they're desperate enough. By kidnapping her pets, the crooks could have forced Maggie into helping them."

"Come on, Dad!" Frank objected. "Maggie wouldn't do something like that. Anyway, why would she ask us to help her find her porpoises if she'd already made a deal with Megavision? And why would she let us stay at her place?"

"To make herself look innocent," his father replied. "Also, she may not trust Megavision to return her pets, so she asked you to find them for her."

"I find that hard to swallow."

"I know. Yet, it can't be entirely ruled out," Mr. Hardy replied. "But first I'll check on Doug Davies. I still think he's our primary suspect."

"What about Joe and Fred?" Frank changed the subject. "Have they called?"

"On that, I have some *good* news," the detective's voice perked up. "I haven't heard from the boys yet, but the police phoned earlier. They have a fix on the two thugs who kidnapped Joe last night and should be able to round them up in a day or so."

"Great!" Frank exclaimed. "At least we'll have a couple of these crooks behind bars."

When he hung up, his head was spinning. Even with all he'd uncovered so far, much remained to be done. Maggie's pets were still missing. The satellite was still missing. Chet was still missing, along with Jason's houseboat. And now, it even seemed possible that Maggie, sweet and attractive as she was, might be a crook after all.

Frank flopped down on one of the easy chairs in Mr. Laker's office and gazed out the window at Fantasieworld. He had some thinking to do!

Joe and Fred, meanwhile, were flying north

over the Intracoastal Waterway. They had followed the route to Miami, near the southernmost tip of mainland Florida, without sighting the aquamarine houseboat. Even if Jason was motoring at a full clip, he couldn't have gone as far as Miami in one day, so they had instructed the pilot to turn around.

Joe anxiously scanned the waterway, which was plainly visible from the air. A number of canals and small rivers branched off it. Jason could have turned on any one of them.

"It would take a week to cover all the side routes," Randy, the pilot, said gloomily. "And if your man headed out into the ocean, it would be like looking for a needle in a haystack."

"Houseboats aren't built for ocean travel," Joe said. "But he may have taken one of the routes inland. All we have to do is figure out which one."

"Oh!" Fred suddenly blurted, slapping his forehead. "Why didn't I think of it before? He probably followed the canal to Lake Okeechobee!"

Joe looked at his friend with a puzzled expression. "What makes you say that?"

"Because that's where I lost the houseboat in the first place!" Fred spoke excitedly. "It was around Stuart, and the canal leading to Okeechobee is just a few miles away. Here, look!"

He spread out an aerial map of the Florida peninsula, and pointed to Lake Okeechobee. A thin blue line showed a narrow channel running clear across the state and connecting the enormous lake to Florida's two coastlines, one on the Atlantic side and the other on the Gulf of Mexico.

"If Jason gets to the Gulf of Mexico, he'll be as hard to find as he'd be in the Atlantic," Joe remarked as he studied the map.

"Yes," Fred agreed. "But he can't make the trip in one day. He'd have to stop along the way for the night, possibly at Okeechobee. That means we could still catch him before he gets to the Gulf."

"Then let's go," Joe said eagerly. "It may be our last chance."

Randy, who had been flying slowly over the waterway, pulled on the control stick and throttled the engines. "I'll have you there in no time," he promised.

They continued north up the waterway until they were above the entrance to the Okeechobee canal. Then they moved westward. Joe

159

and Fred peered anxiously out their windows, searching the narrow strip of water for a sign of the houseboat. By the time they reached the lake, however, they still had not discovered it.

"Let's loop around," Joe suggested.

They searched the perimeter of the large inland lake. Much of its banks were covered with dense trees and foliage, and only a smattering of roads led into the area. Houses were few and far between.

When they were almost halfway around, Joe's eyes suddenly fixed on a tiny cove. It was shrouded by a cluster of mangrove trees hanging over the water in a thick confusion of branches. Through the leaves, the sun glinted off something large and aquamarine!

"I think I see it," he breathed, and pointed toward the cove.

Randy made a low pass over the cove. The boxlike object was indeed Jason's houseboat, hidden well beneath the mangrove branches! Near it, nestled in a clearing behind the trees, were a few small shacks. But there were no roads leading to the cove at all. The only way to reach it was by water.

"We've got to get a boat," Joe said urgently. "Do you know where we can land?"

The pilot looked at his two young passengers

with a wide grin. "No. But I have a better idea. Do either of you know how to use a parachute?"

"Yes," Joe replied. "But how could I—"

"There's an open, grassy area about a mile behind us," Randy interrupted. "I could drop you off there, and you could walk to the cove to keep an eye on the houseboat. In the meantime, I'll fly back to the Space Center and trade this plane in for one with pontoons. Then Fred and I can come down on the lake and join you. It won't take more than an hour or so. I'll land farther along the cove over there, so Jason doesn't see me."

"Great!" Joe agreed. "I'll meet you there in an hour."

On the pilot's instructions, he grabbed a parachute pack from a compartment behind the backseat. Although he was no expert sky diver, he had taken a course in parachute jumping the summer before and knew the basics. He strapped the chute on and opened the door to the aircraft.

Once they were directly over the grassy area, Randy cut his engines. "Okay . . . Jump!" he shouted.

Joe let go of the doorframe and dropped. A few seconds later, the parachute billowed out above him like a giant mushroom and he gently floated to the ground.

After landing, Joe waved at the plane to indicate he was all right, then watched as it flew out of sight. He gathered up the parachute and hiked down the shore toward the cove. The houseboat was still there. If Jason decided to leave now, at least Joe would know which direction their suspect would take.

But the young detective was too impatient to just watch and wait. He circled around the cove to get a closer look. The collection of shacks had intrigued him the moment he saw them. Maybe Jason wasn't only using this spot as a stopover on his way to the Gulf of Mexico. Perhaps this was where he stored his illegal merchandise!

Keeping a wary eye on the houseboat, Joe stepped into the clearing and stealthily made his way to the largest shack.

Before going in, he quickly scanned the area to make sure Jason was not in sight. Then, his heart pumping with anticipation, he slowly pushed open the door. Would Chet be there, tied up in a corner?

18 Underwater Surprise

The door swung open and Joe stared in surprise. There was no sign of Chet or Jason. There was nothing but a big fish tank, filling the entire interior of the shack!

There were sharks, rays, barracudas, and other fish, swimming lazily about in the water, which Joe judged to be about fifteen feet deep.

"So this is where he keeps his cache of stolen animals!" the boy murmured. He peered at the assortment of captive creatures for a few more moments, then left the shack to check out the other buildings in the clearing. They housed more fish tanks and a collection of nets, poles, pullies, and other gear which the thief apparently used to capture the animals. None of the tanks, however, contained Sam and Samantha. There were no porpoises at all.

Sadly, Joe left the clearing and hid within a clump of bushes. *I bet he already sold Maggie's pets,* the boy thought as he kept an eye on the houseboat. Some minutes passed; then he saw Jason emerge from the houseboat, carrying a bucket in each hand. They were filled to the brim with dead fish. It was feeding time!

As Joe watched, Jason carried the buckets from one shack to the next. *He steals the animals with his blue van,* Joe figured. *It must be equipped with a small saltwater tank. But he can hardly keep them alive very long in a little container. How does he get them all the way to Lake Okeechobee?*

Suddenly he had an idea. *It has to be the houseboat!* Joe told himself, remembering that there were no roads leading to the isolated cove. *But we searched it just yesterday, and there was no place Jason kept a—*

The amateur detective caught himself in mid-sentence as the answer suddenly flashed into his mind—it accounted not only for how the animals were transported, but also for where Chet probably was at this very moment!

"Why didn't we think of it before?" he beamed, snapping his fingers with glee.

Waiting anxiously for feeding time to be over, he watched Jason return to his houseboat and go inside. As soon as the cabin door was shut, Joe stripped down to his undershorts and crept through the mangrove trees to the water's edge. He took a deep breath and dropped below the surface.

He swam underwater until he was beneath the bow of the houseboat. There he came up for a moment, drew another breath and ducked down again, this time swimming directly beneath the hull of the boat. What he saw nearly caused him to blow out his air in a gasp of horror.

The center of the houseboat's hull was hollowed out to form a big underwater cage. And through a latticework of aluminum bars, Joe could make out the chubby profile of Chet's body!

At first, the blond-haired sleuth thought Chet had drowned. But then he noticed that there was a narrow pocket of air between the water and the floor of the boat. It was no more than a foot high, but it gave Chet enough room to keep his head above the surface and breathe. From

his neck down, though, the chubby boy was underwater, standing on the aluminum grating at the bottom of the cage.

There was no way Joe could break through the bars to rescue his friend. He would have to get into the houseboat, overcome Jason, then find the trapdoor leading to the tank. But Joe could at least tug on Chet's shoe to let him know he was soon to be rescued from his makeshift torture chamber!

At first, the chubby youth thought it was a big fish nibbling on his foot, and he jerked away. But when he looked down and saw Joe, he had to stifle a cry of relief. With hand motions, Joe gestured that he would be back, then swam away, unable to hold his breath any longer.

After surfacing for a moment, Joe swam underwater as long as he could toward the far side of the cove. Then he climbed up on the bank. He marched along the edge, soaking wet, to meet Randy and Fred. The two were already waiting for him and had brought Frank along.

"What happened to you?" Frank asked in surprise when he saw his brother.

"I found Chet!" Joe panted. "The houseboat has an underwater cage built into its hull. Jason's been using it to transport the stolen sea animals to those shacks here, and now he's keeping Chet in it!"

"So *that's* where he was!" Fred cried. Then his face darkened. "Is he okay?"

"I think so," Joe replied. "I swam beneath the houseboat and could see him standing up in the cage. His head was out of the water, and when I got his attention, he recognized me. But I'll bet he's plenty tired, plenty scared, and plenty waterlogged."

"Let's get him out of there right away!" Frank exclaimed.

Randy and the three boys went toward the cove. On the way, Joe told about the fish tanks he had found in the shacks.

The foursome rounded the cove, staying hidden within the gnarled confusion of mangrove trees. When they were near the houseboat, Joe picked up his clothes in the bushes and quickly put them on. Then he led the way as they jumped aboard the houseboat and kicked open its door!

Taken by surprise, Jason leaped across his cabin and grabbed the spear gun from the wall. He aimed it at Joe's body and fired!

Joe, however, was prepared for the assault. He lunged to the floor the instant the spear was released. It hit the wall with a sharp crack, its

168

deadly point sinking deeply into the wood paneling.

The red-haired thief was now defenseless. "If you guys lay one hand on me, you'll never see your friend alive," he hissed, backing into a corner. "I guarantee it."

Without a word, Frank and Fred flew across the cabin and pinned Jason to the wall. While they held him securely, Joe and the pilot stripped a large rug from the center of the floor. Underneath was the trapdoor. And under the trapdoor was Chet!

The chubby boy was too weak to pull himself out of the underwater cage. It was all he could do to raise his arms through the opening and have Joe and Randy hoist him up.

"I thought I was a goner," Chet choked, tearfully happy to see his friends again. His skin was shriveled and he was shivering. Joe led him to a chair while Randy looked for a blanket to wrap around Chet.

"Were you in that tank for two days?" Joe asked.

"No," Chet replied. "He only put me there when we were docked. I wouldn't have survived otherwise! I don't think I would have lasted much longer as it was!"

Joe patted him on the shoulder. "We

wouldn't let you down, old buddy," he said with a smile. "After all, it's our duty to protect friendly sea cows. They're an endangered species, you know."

Chet cracked a thin grin at Joe's kidding. "I'm so shriveled up I *feel* like a sea cow," he said, looking at his arms. "I hope my skin doesn't stay this way, or everyone will think I'm an old man!"

"I'm just glad we got you in time," Fred spoke up. "I felt awful about losing you." Then he glanced at Jason, who was struggling to free himself and cursing under his breath.

"What'll we do with him?" he asked. "Tie him up?"

"Let's give him a taste of his own medicine," Frank suggested, "and put him in the tank!"

"Good idea!" Joe chimed in.

Taking the struggling and screaming villain by his arms and legs, the foursome lifted him and dropped him through the trapdoor. Then they closed its lid, shutting the redheaded crook in his own watery prison.

"How long are you planning to leave him there?" Randy asked.

"Oh, just for a little while," Frank said. "Then we'll ask him some questions!"

The boys found dry clohes for Chet to put on

and made him a cup of tea. After a half hour, they let Jason out again and asked him about Maggie's pets. The man, however, refused to talk.

"I suppose this wasn't long enough," Frank said, and locked the criminal up again.

"You'll pay for this!" Jason screamed. "Someday I'm going to get you and drown you all!"

19   A Scandal

Frank found the housboat's radio-telephone and contacted the Coast Guard. Soon a patrol boat entered the cove and two officers boarded the houseboat. Frank reported what had happend, then showed the officers the shacks.

"This is incredible!" one of them said. "Who would have ever looked in this forsaken place for stolen animals! You boys did a great job!"

The Coast Guard took Jason into custody and said they would return to recover the houseboat and the animals once he was safely in prison.

After they had left, the boys and Randy piled into the airplane, and soon the pontooned craft was soaring over the waters of Lake Okeechobee on an easterly course. The sun was setting behind them and by the time they landed at the Space Center, night had fallen.

Fred volunteered to take Chet home, since the chubby boy needed rest more than anything. Randy said good-bye to the group, and the Hardys, after thanking him for his help, went inside to meet their father, who was working around the clock with the security people.

"I'm glad Chet's all right," Mr. Hardy said with a sigh of relief after hearing his sons' story. "Now I have some good news for you, too. I checked up on Maggie and Mr. Davies while you were gone, and it's beginning to look as if Davies may be our man."

"What did you find out?" Joe asked.

"One of the security guards here told me that on the day prior to the launch he let Davies make one final inspection of the satellite. It wasn't normal procedure, but the designer insisted on checking something. So the guard let him in. Davies was left alone with the satellite for some time, and nobody recalls having seen him leave."

"Are you saying he hid somewhere and stayed overnight?" Frank asked.

"I don't know. On the day of the launch, Davies told everyone he had checked satellite in the space capsule himself. None of the other technicians saw the satellite after he made his final inspection, so he could have taken it out."

"Was the satellite light enough for one man to handle?" Joe inquired.

The sleuth's father nodded. "That was the part that's unique about Davies's new design. There has never been one like that before."

"What do you think he did with it?" Frank spoke up.

"He may have carried it away to some hiding place, and then, after the launch, when security was loosened, he may have hauled it away unnoticed. Problem is, we need proof!"

"How are we going to get it?"

"I contacted Mr. Laker at Fantasieworld," the detective replied. "He has agreed to let Maggie go there tonight and run tests on the Bear Dance computer. She may be able to tell whether it was used to make up a program to work in conjunction with an emulator during the launch."

Just then, Maggie appeared, walking quickly toward the group. She looked pleadingly at Frank and Joe. "Did you have any luck in finding Sam and Samantha?" she asked.

"Not yet," Frank admitted, feeling embarrassed at having to dash her hopes once again. "We know who stole them, and how it was done, but we haven't figured out where the pets are."

"All we've managed to do is to wreck your motorcycle," Joe said, looking depressed.

"Oh, that's all right," Maggie said. "You could've been killed, and all that really counts is that you're okay."

"We'd better be going to Fantasieworld," Mr. Hardy said, looking at his watch. "Mr. Laker will be waiting for us."

They all piled into Maggie's pickup truck and drove to the amusement park, stopping on the way only to have a quick hamburger. When they arrived, Mr. Laker was standing outside the front gate. Through the employees' entrance, he led them into the maze of underground tunnels. It was now almost deserted except for a few watchmen on duty.

"Here we are," Mr. Laker said and stopped at the computer room that Frank had visited earlier. Maggie went right to work. She ran a series of tests, and data from its memory banks flashed across the screen as she pushed buttons and adjusted dials.

Frank and Joe, meanwhile, searched the

175

room for clues. Printouts were piled high on shelves, and files were stuffed in drawers. Methodically, the young detectives went through everything.

After some time had elapsed, Maggie sat back in her chair and shrugged. "This computer could do it," she announced. "But if there was any special program run on it, it has been completely erased."

"Wait a second," Frank spoke up. He pulled a tape out of one of the drawers and held it to the light. It had been stuck under a pile of papers, and on it were written the initials *A.S.* "These might stand for Aristo Satellite," he said excitedly, handing the tape to Maggie.

The pretty technician eagerly loaded the program tape into the computer. A few seconds later her eyes grew wide as she stared at the data screen. "This is it!" she cried with glee. "This is the exact same information readout the satellite is supposed to give for the launch!"

"Great," Fenton Hardy smiled. "It's the proof we needed."

Maggie took off the program and handed it to Mr. Hardy, who stuffed it into his briefcase.

The only one in the room who wasn't elated by the news was the personnel manager. "Does this mean our computer operator, Larry Web, is guilty of sabotage?" he groaned.

"I'm afraid it does," Frank replied sympathetically. "It looks like both Mr. Web and Buster were hired to help out in this scheme. And as soon as we nail the top man, we're going to have them arrested. I'm sure it won't tarnish Fantasieworld's image. Any organization can be penetrated by a criminal."

Mr. Laker threw up his hands. "I can just see it now: FANTASIEWORLD COMPUTER USED IN THEFT OF SATELLITE! All over the newspapers. It will be a scandal. A scandal!"

Assuring the agitated man that they would try to keep the amusement park's name out of the papers, Frank, Joe, and Mr. Hardy left the computer room and returned with Maggie to her pickup truck.

"What's our next step?" Joe asked. "Do we confront Davies with this tape?"

"I think we should confront him, but not accuse him," Frank spoke up. "We'll let him know that we're on to the scheme, but pretend not to suspect *him*. This may make him nervous enough so he'll make a mistake. Perhaps not right away, but in the near future."

Mr. Hardy nodded. "That sounds like a good

plan. And I think you boys should do it alone. Davies has rented a cottage not far from Cocoa Beach. I'll give you his address and the tape; then you can take it from there."

The plan was set. Instead of calling in the police, Frank and Joe would visit Davies. At the Space Center, they took down his address and soon were on their way.

It was now close to midnight and the designer would probably be in bed. But that would be good, the boys reasoned. Davies would be too tired and surprised to think clearly.

Frank and Joe followed a road to the north end of Cocoa Beach. They soon found the cottage, and as they'd expected, it was dark. Only a front porch light was on. The two youths pounded on the door until they saw another light come on inside.

"Who is it?" a gruff, male voice demanded through the door.

"It's Frank and Joe Hardy!" Frank replied urgently. "May we come in?"

The boys heard the latch click. Then the door swung open and Davies stuck his head out. He was wearing a bathrobe and slippers. "What do you kids want at this hour?" he yawned irritatedly. "Do you know it's after midnight? I was asleep."

"We're sorry," Frank apologized. "But this is important. It's about the Aristo satellite."

A suspicious look crept over the designer's face, but he quickly hid it behind a false smile. "Did you find out what happened to it?" he asked, pretending to be eager.

"No. But we think we're on the right track," Joe replied. "We've been investigating a couple of stolen porpoises, and we believe we've stumbled on to something that ties in with the satellite. So we thought we'd get your advice on it."

The designer was still smiling, but when he spoke his voice sounded nervous. "Then come on in," he said, stepping aside to let the youths pass. "Let's hear about this discovery of yours."

Frank and Joe entered the cottage and sat down on the living room sofa. They waited until Davies was also seated before saying anything.

"We found this at Fantasiewold," Frank said finally as he drew the computer program tape from his jacket. "It is a phony program of the satellite launch. This proves that someone stole the satellite before the launch ever took place . . . someone who had access to the satellite and the Space Center computer."

Davies froze in his seat, trying to control a rush of fright!

20 An Amazing Discovery

Finally the designer pulled himself together and feigned surprise at the news.

"That's amazing!" he squeaked, overplaying his delight. "You're saying that someone at Fantasieworld actually made up a program to interface with a space craft emulator to fool everyone into believing that the satellite was fine, when, in fact, it had been stolen before it left the ground?"

"That's right," Frank said. "This tape proves it."

"Amazing," Davies repeated. "I never would've imagined it possible." He then looked warily at the two boys. "Do you have any idea who it was, or how they managed to steal it? Megavision seems like the best bet to me."

"That's why we came to you," Joe said. "Better than anyone, you know how the satellite was designed and how it could have been stolen. So we wanted your opinion on it."

Davies stood up. "I'll sleep on it tonight and get back to you in the morning," he said seriously. "You boys have been a tremendous help, and together we'll get to the bottom of it very soon. But I'm sure it has to be Megavision. That first sabotage attempt was probably just a ploy to divert everyone's attention while those crooks stole the satellite right out from under our noses. And I bet they bribed somebody at Fantasieworld to work up that phony program."

Frank and Joe also stood up, and the designer ushered them to the front door.

"You're probably right about Megavision," Frank remarked on the way out. "But the police will be checking out everyone who could've gotten near the satellite. Even you. We can talk about that in the morning, though."

"Yes. In the morning." Davies spoke in a strained manner, shaking the Hardys' hands.

Frank and Joe left the house and walked back to their pickup.

"Boy, that guy's nervous," Joe said as he

climbed in. "His hand felt like a wet sponge when I shook it."

"Good," Frank grinned. "That's just the way we want him."

He started the pickup and drove down the street. Then he pulled to the curb and parked. The boys doubled back on foot and hid in the dark outside the cottage.

The lights were still on. A half hour later, a truck stopped in front of the house and two men got out. They were the two Fantasieworld employees, Buster and the computer operator, Larry Web! They disappeared inside the cottage.

"We'll need help," Frank whispered to his brother. "Drive to the Space Center and get Dad and a couple of security men."

Joe nodded and disappeared. Mr Hardy had promised to wait until he'd heard from his sons, and there would be guards at the Space Center. Together, they would outumber Davies and his two accomplices. But would they get there in time?

Frank continued to spy on the cottage from behind a hedge. Through the windows he could see the three men moving about. Then the door suddenly opened, revealing a wooden crate in the entrance hall.

The three men lifted the crate and carried it outside.

"Come on!" Frank muttered, anxiously looking down the street for the pickup. In another minute, the men and the crate would be gone!

Luckily, just as Davies and his cohorts were about halfway to the truck, Maggie's pickup appeared at the end of the street. It was followed by a Space Center security car. The two vehicles screeched to a stop in front of the cottage and Mr. Hardy, Joe, and three armed guards piled out.

"What's going on!" Davies cried out, dropping the crate.

The three criminals tried to run away, but were captured and subdued in short order. Then, after finding a crowbar in back of the pickup, Frank and Joe pried open the lid of the wooden crate. Inside was the missing Aristo satellite! It resembled a huge flashlight battery with a circular antenna hinged at one end, giving it the appearance of a half-open can. Part of the cylinder was covered with glistening solar cells.

Frank looked quizzically at Davies, who was now handcuffed and in the grip of a security man.

"How much did Megavision pay you to

sabotage this instrument that you built your-
self?"

Doug Davies looked defeated. His face suddenly seemed ten years older and his shoulders
sagged. "Megavision had nothing to do with it,"
he said.

"What!" the Hardys cried out in unison.

"I found that there was a design flaw in the
satellite," Davies went on. "But I didn't know it
until it was finished and being tested. It . . . it
would have destroyed the instrument soon after
it reached its orbit. And . . . it would have destroyed the reputation of my company."

Davies took a deep breath. "I know you will
think I was only concerned about myself. But
that isn't true. Super Tech is a relatively new
company with a great future and a great staff.
With the Aristo satellite a failure, they would
have gone out of business."

"I don't understand," Joe said. "Couldn't you
have rectified the problem and delayed the
launch?"

Davies shook his head. "Impossible. We
started out from the wrong premise when we
determined the basic design. We needed time
to rethink our theory and have a chance to build
a new instrument. With the stiff competition
going on in this field, there was no way to do

that. I wanted to buy time—time for Super Tech, and everyone connected with it. Yes, for myself, too."

The man paused a moment, too choked up to go on. Then he said, "As long as everyone thought the Aristo satellite was destroyed by a killer satellite we could have collected the insurance money, stayed in business and tried again." He shrugged. "It was not to be."

"So you hired Larry Web," Frank said. "What did you offer to pay him to keep his mouth shut?"

"Nothing," Davies said. "Larry and I are old friends."

Web cleared his throat. "I didn't want the company to go under, either. We ... we all started a couple of years ago and practically created it. When we realized what happened, we came up with the solution. I went to work for Fantasieland, where I knew I would have access to a suitable computer."

"And when you were confronted with the problem of getting Maggie away from her station long enough to input the phony program, you got Buster to help," Joe said.

"We didn't anticipate that problem," Davies said. "I thought I could handle the computer matter. When I couldn't, Larry suggested getting in touch with Buster. He had once worked at Sealand and had friends in the business of stealing animals. He arranged for the kidnapping, hiring Jason Meld for the job."

"Did you stay at the Space Center the night before the launch?" Frank asked.

Davies nodded. "I hid the satellite in one of the storerooms and removed it later."

"What happened to Maggie's porpoises?" Mr. Hardy inquired. "They weren't with the batch of animals that Meld was going to sell."

"When he moved them from the van into the houseboat, they got away. He didn't have any help that time and couldn't handle them by himself."

The boys' faces fell. "Now Maggie'll never get them back," Joe said sadly.

The security guards now led the designer and his confederates to their car.

The Hardys spent the night on makeshift cots at the Space Center, and in the morning they met Fred and Chet at Maggie's house to tell her what had happened. They found the pretty technician at her lagoon, happily watching two porpoises swimming about.

"You . . . you got new ones?" Frank asked, surprised.

"No!" Maggie laughed. "Sam and Samantha

came back this morning! I went to the beach and there they were, trying to get into the lagoon!"

"Terrific!" Joe cried out. "We learned last night that they got away from the man who had stolen them, and thought they were gone for good."

"All the crooks are behind bars, by the way," Frank added. "Including Doug Davies, who engineered the disappearance of the satellite because of a design flaw." Quickly he filled Maggie in on the latest developments.

"It's amazing," she said when he finished. "And you not only figured out his clever scheme but caught him with the goods! I'm going to fix you all a big breakfast as a reward. Then I'll give you boys the best ride you ever had!"

With that, she ran into the house. Frank and Joe looked at each other, puzzled.

"What do you think she's up to?" Fred wondered.

"I don't know," Mr. Hardy said. "But let's go inside. I want to make some phone calls before we eat."

He found out from the police that Skip Adkins had been arrested that morning. So had the two thugs Megavision had hired to kill Joe.

When he told the others while they were having blueberry pancakes, everyone cheered loudly.

"Now there's only one mystery left," Joe said. "Maggie, how about telling us about that ride?"

"As soon as you're finished eating," she said with a twinkle in her eyes.

Half an hour later, all stood in front of the lagoon again. "Now," Maggie said. "Who wants to be the first to go on the world-famous Sam and Samantha porpoise ride?"

"You mean—on their backs?" Chet asked, his eyes popping.

"That's right! I've done it many times. It's loads of fun."

"I'll go!" Frank said.

"Then jump in and grab a fin!"

Frank and Joe simultaneously took off their shoes and socks and dove into the water. In seconds, Sam and Samantha were beside them. With Maggie shouting instructions from the shore, the boys grabbed the porpoises' back fins and mounted them like horses. The young detectives deserved some fun, because soon they would be called upon another case, called *The Roaring River Mystery*.

Sam and Samantha were carrying the youths in circles around the lagoon.

"It's like an aquatic bronco ride!" Mr. Hardy chortled as he watched his sons fall off and get on again. "Hey, I'm coming in, too!"

Fred followed the detective and the four took turns riding the porpoises.

"Chet, don't you want to join us?" Joe yelled at their chubby friend, who was still ashore.

Chet shook his head. "Oh, no. After my experience in Jason's cage, I never want to get wet again in my whole life!"